LADY LIESL'S SEASIDE SURPRISE

TANSY RAYNER ROBERTS

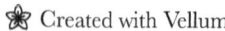

For Emma, with her attitudes
And Lizzie, who did not drown

CONTENTS

FOREWORD

Lady Liesl's Seaside Surprise belongs to the Teacup Magic series, and also stands alone.

We first met Liesl as a supporting character in the first two cozy mystery adventures of Miss Mnemosyne Seabourne: *Tea and Sympathetic Magic* and *The Frost Fair Affair*. This story happens during the same summer as *Spellcracker's Honeymoon*.

DRAMATIS PERSONAE

THE FAMILY

LADY LIESL OF SANDWICH, *a plucky young lady, unmarried after two Seasons*

GEORGE BATTENBURG-SEVILLE, EARL OF SANDWICH, *patron of the arts (recent), father to Liesl*

EMMA LAMB BATTENBURG-SEVILLE, COUNTESS OF SANDWICH, *actress-turned-aristocrat, stepmother to Liesl*

LADY ANNABETHA (ANNA) BATTENBURG-SEVILLE CHISHOLM, *wife of a country Baronet, elder sister to Liesl*

LADY MARGARETTA (RETTA) BATTERNBURG-SEVILLE SOTHEBY, *wife of a Lord, elder sister to Liesl*

LADY GERDRUT (GERDA) BATTENBURG-SEVILLE MELUSINE, *wife of a wealthy banker, elder sister to Liesl*

GUSTAV BATTENBURG-SEVILLE, VISCOUNT
GANYMEDE, *bachelor heir to the Earl of Sandwich, elder
brother to Liesl*

LADY CLYTIE BATTENBURG-SEVILLE, *schoolgirl and
correspondent, younger sister to Liesl*

THE BOHEMIANS

BASIL ROBUCKS, *famous art critic, infamous clothes horse*

PERDITA CHOLMONDLEY, *up and coming artist with a
taste for marble and a talent for paint*

INDIGO LARKIN, *artist's model who seems to model herself
on others; pond-survivor*

MEREDITH (MERRY) MERRYWEATHER, *self-styled poet
king; on the verge of his greatest work*

STAFF, AND OTHERS

AMIE, *a lady's maid*

MR TORQUAY, *a butler*

TAVISTOCK, *a maid of all work*

MRS PENNANCE, *a cook with a theatrical past*

EVANS, *valet to Basil Robucks*

BETS, *a tweeny*

OF BRIGHTSIDE AND CURRICLES

FROM: *LADY LIESL BATTENBURG-SEVILLE OF SANDWICH, APHRODITE VILLA, BRIGHTSIDE, THE ISLE OF BATH*

TO: *MRS MNEMOSYNE SEABOURNE, COMFREY COTTAGE, MUDGELY, THE ISLE OF ASTER*

*M*y dear Mneme,

Now you are married to the love of your life and blissfully happy, I expect you to provide those of us who remain on the shelf with your experience and knowledge.

Which is to say, I have attached a list of highly pertinent (or merely pert) questions that only a matron could possibly answer. I await your return letter with bated breath. Please devote especial attention to the third and sixth questions, for educational purposes.

Naturally, you have nothing more important to do on

your honeymoon than share your intimate secrets with your maidenly friends! You may blush now, but within a twelve-month you shall surely be scrawling tell-all novels about married life to be shared with a discreet group, as all my old school chums seem to have done.

Mind you, scandalous novels about marital (and extra-marital) affairs was the fashion last Season. These days they all seem to have turned their hands to mysteries: tales of heiresses and governesses stranded in unfamiliar houses, doing their best to solve overly-complicated crimes while trying not to fall in love with seductive rakes. I assume all this novel-writing means that the second year of marriage is otherwise dull and uneventful. Rest assured, I shall have a further list of questions for you by the time you reach that sorry state.

I may be about to embark on a short adventure of my own, though it is nothing warranting a honeymoon. Do not be surprised if your reply to my letter is forwarded to a mysterious location.

And of course, my dear Mneme, do not allow this detour to deter you from answering Question 7 in intimate detail. Illustrations are positively encouraged.

Your friend,
Liesl

～

*L*ady Liesl Battenburg-Seville was on the wrong side of the island, to begin with.

It was all very well that ladies were allowed to use portals now — already she thought of her life as divided between Portals and No Portals, with the latter a haze of swan-shaped boats and ungainly lumps of luggage

BERT, *a stable lad*

A helpful post-mistress

An unhelpful if accurate secretary

Assorted townies

THE CORRESPONDENTS, LIVING AND DECEASED

ANA-MARGARETA DANVILLE BATTENBURG-SEVILLE, FORMER COUNTESS OF SANDWICH, *(deceased) mother of Liesl and her siblings*

GERDRUTTE TALBOY BATTENBURG-SEVILLE, FORMER DOWAGER COUNTESS OF SANDWICH, *(deceased) mother of George, grandmother of Liesl and her siblings*

MRS MNEMOSYNE "MNEME" SEABOURNE, *a dear friend and correspondent, occasional solver of mysteries*

LADY MARGERY FOULKKES-HOBB, VISCOUNTESS DUDLEY, *an old school friend and correspondent, prolific mystery novelist*

JUNO, DUCHESS OF STORM, *a dear friend and correspondent, confirmed meddler in mysteries*

HENRY, DUKE OF STORM, *the one who got away*

being touted back and forth — but it was another thing to use them with any degree of expertise.

She thought she had done the right thing, consulting with her father's secretary, who she assumed would know the most convenient way to access the family villa on the coast of Bath. However, when Liesl stepped out of the portal, accompanied by one highly-strung maid holding a carpet bag, she discovered that she was still at least two hours travel away from her intended destination.

Dismay was the only possible reaction.

"This is the north side of the island, my dear," explained a kindly post-mistress. "You need to be on the east, oh quite far down the coast to reach Brightside. Surely there must be an inn or a respectable establishment closer to the town with a portal available to ladies… hmm, let me look."

And yet, after the post-mistress consulted all of the information to hand, it transpired that Lady Liesl's father's secretary had not been incorrect. This was the nearest public portal.

Amie, Liesl's maid, was on the verge of tears.

The predicted two hours of travel was closer to three by the time they had hired a two-wheeled curricle to the station, caught a little train that wound in and out of various coastal villages, and finally hired a second curricle to take them up high over the curve of the cliffs towards the town of Brightside where, Liesl was assured, the villa was to be found.

This was not a Bath she recognised from regular child-hood visits to the other side of the island: all the spa resorts and theatres and delightful amusements around every corner. No, this was all moors and cliff and chilly isolation.

What had her father been thinking?

There was little brightness to be had by the time they approached Aphrodite Villa, named for the goddess of love. Liesl's fair hair and favourite bonnet were so blown about by the curricle that they had formed some kind of unholy tangle that might require divine intervention to unravel. Amie clung to the side of the small carriage, pale and miserably travel-sick.

Given that the sun rose in the east, the brightness of Brightside must be a pleasure to be enjoyed in the mornings. Certainly not an hour or so after the last civilised hour for tea.

Summer it might be, but there was little warmth in the air. All colour had bleached out of the sea and the sky in preparation for evening. Liesl should have packed a more robust shawl in her — she was now starting to realise — entirely unsatisfactory carpet bag. Spoiled by a few months of easy portal travel, she had forgotten how to properly pack.

At least, *surely*, her visit to Aphrodite Villa would be brief. She had a single message to deliver on behalf of her father, after which she could return home to prepare for the next Season with her conscience clear.

Ugh. Next Season. The least thought about that, the better.

"I'm not here to solve a mystery," she said aloud, causing Amie to give her a startled look.

She must start as she meant to go on.

And that, Liesl decided as she passed the care of her hired horse over to a helpful passing stable lad, included not wondering *at all* why exactly it was that this particular villa, purchased by her father upon his second marriage, was so very difficult to reach.

She had read enough mystery novels to know exactly where that sort of question led.

Even in the unflattering light of early evening,

4

Aphrodite Villa was somewhat impressive. Liesl had never visited the property before, as it was the private sanctum of her father and stepmother from the moment their months-long honeymoon began. None of the children of his first marriage had been invited here in the six years since that second wedding; not even Gustav, the son and heir.

~

*D*ear Mamma,
    You won't believe what Father did the moment you were dead.

~

"*B*ig, isn't it?" gasped Amie at her side, clutching the carpet bag with a dedicated fervour.

That was one word for it.

Liesl could see she could see why the whole business had put Gustav in a grim mood when the purchase was first announced. Far from being a modest holiday house fit for an Earl and his much younger wife, this was a magnificently grand establishment, almost as large as their own family manor, Battenburg Abbey. Unlike the Abbey with its forbidding thick buttresses and solid two-centuries-ago design, this flighty Aphrodite Villa was built of white granite, with wide sweeping steps and thick columns holding up a majestic portico with a colonnade that swept the entire perimeter of the house, it looked almost palatial.

Certainly, it must contain enough rooms for Liesl and all five of her siblings to be housed comfortably, should they ever be invited to stay.

Beyond the deep white portico, the front door stood wide open. A sound of flute music could be heard from within, along with the chatter of a crowd. A party, perhaps? Liesl stepped inside, looking around for someone she could talk to about sleeping arrangements. It was generally best to manage rooms and such with the servants before giving her host a chance to notice she had arrived.

There were no servants in sight. Only tiles: a glorious mosaic floor that swept across a hallway wide enough to double as a ballroom. Blue and white and blue and white, in an intricate pattern that formed waves and seashell patterns, using turned sea glass as well as fine china in various brilliant shades. Beautiful. Expensive.

Also, the ultimate sign of casual wealth: there was not a grain of dust or dirt anywhere, and yet no scent of cleaning charms hung in the air. That meant it was cleaned entirely by hand.

A door flew open, and the most beautiful woman Liesl had ever seen in her life stormed out of it, arguing over one bare shoulder. She had eyes like a cat, large and perfectly-shaped. Her long dark hair was caught up in a careless knot, and she wore a draping white gown that was almost entirely indecent in the way it fell around her curves and long limbs. "I'm telling you, Basil, it's entirely the wrong shade of carmine," she hollered like a fishwife, as the door swung shut behind her. There was no Basil in sight.

The woman in the indecent dress saw Liesl and tilted her head with a slow smile. "Well, hello," she said, prowling in Liesl's general direction. "Are you the enter-tainment?"

Liesl froze in place, the social awkwardness of her early teen years swamping back over her, as if it had never been away. This was not a situation on which she had been drilled by her army of governesses, or her brutally effective finishing school. "I'm looking for the Countess of Sandwich," she managed, her discomfort affecting her tone as it always did: making her appear icy, aloof.

The sensuous woman held her gaze for a touch longer than was polite, then stepped back and opened the door again. "Emma!" she yelled into the flute music and conversational hum. "Someone's sent you an angel! Bags I paint her first."

2

AN IMPROPER COUNTESS

Someone's sent you an angel. Liesl had never been introduced to a room with such a sentiment before. She hovered on the threshold, flushed with embarrassment.

"Are you going in, or running away?" purred the indecently-draped woman.

That was useful; Liesl was annoyed now. She straightened her spine. "I don't run from anything."

"Oh, good. That would be no fun at all."

Braced for the most extravagant display of scandalous decadence, given everything she had heard about her stepmother's friends, Liesl stepped into the sitting room.

It was hardly a surprise that the room was beautiful, decorated grandly in the current fashion. Unlike the blazing whites and blues of the hallway, this room was warmer in tone, with creams and reds and a striped pattern of roses on the walls.

A mighty, gold-framed portrait of the Earl and his new Countess hung above the fireplace. She, accomplished actress that she was, looked every inch the aristocratic wife: fashionably gowned and dripping with ancestral diamonds. He stood, as awkward in oils as he was in real life, with one hand set upon her shoulder, and many layers of tweed between himself and his wife.

It was almost a relief to see that he still came off badly in portraits; Liesl never quite knew what to expect of her father these days. The Old Earl had been distant, aloof, cold. Weighed down by generations of tradition and social expectation. The New Earl threw wild parties, made friends with artists and poets. He disappeared for months at a time without informing his family where he might be found, and when he returned, it was with a new wife at his side.

Gone to Bohemia, as Liesl's late grandmamma might have said, sniffing her disapproval. *No forwarding address.*

Gallivanting, as Liesl's late mother might have said, rolling her eyes. *Honestly, Bats, isn't there enough to do around here?*

∾

*D*ear Mamma
    Look at me, playing the dutiful daughter just because the Earl deigned to ask me for a favour.

(He didn't ask, actually. He assumed.)

∾

*U*nlike her stately formal portrait, the current Countess of Sandwich was dressed in a pale blue day-dress stained with paint. She wore no jewellery except her wedding ring and a rustic-looking charm bracelet. Her feet were scandalously bare — bad enough to appear this way in private where only the servants might see her, but she had a man sitting on either side of her, and a young woman (equally barefoot!) sitting on the floor nearby, like an urchin begging for bread off the table.

Liesl was quite certain that no man — not even her father or brother — had seen her own bare feet since she was six or seven years old.

"An angel indeed," leered one of the men, who had a dark pointed beard and a gleam in his eye. He wore a baggy brown shirt tied with a cord, like he had wandered in from the market selling eels, and decided to stay for the rest of his life. "I'll fight you for her, Perdita."

"Don't be an ass," said Emma, a laugh in her voice. "This is my daughter."

That was unexpected. "Stepdaughter," Liesl corrected quickly.

"Of course," said Emma, her smile unwavering. She held out both her hands to Liesl. "I'm so glad to see you. Don't be offended by my friends. We're all rather casual here."

"I was hardly expecting a formal cotillion," Liesl managed to sound amused rather than shocked or scandalised. "Though it's quite the house for it." She allowed Emma to squeeze her hands and draw her down next to her on the settee; a beautifully dressed man in an iris-coloured jacket and matching pantaloons slid aside to make room for her.

"I forgot you hadn't been here before," said Emma with a laugh. "Isn't it a disgrace? So many pillars, and enough bedrooms to start a hotel."

"Are you checking in?" asked the throaty woman with the cat's eyes. She lounged in the doorway, watching the scene.

Liesl felt entirely scrutinised, as if the slightest wrong move would have her immortalised in satirical poetry, or a rude cartoon. "I was hoping to stay a little while," she said.

"You're always welcome here," said Emma, Countess of Sandwich.

"Ask what she wants, first," said the other woman. "The price might be too high."

Emma shot her friend a warning look. "Don't be rude, Perdita. Honestly, you'd think you were all brought up in a barn."

"I do need to speak to you about a private matter," Liesl said, feeling a touch apologetic. It had never really occurred to her to call upon her stepmother until she was given a specific mission to do so.

For the first time, the blazing smile of the Countess faltered a little. "And I suppose it's not something to be said in front of my friends?" she asked, a little wryly.

"I'd rather keep it between us us," said Liesl.

"And there you are," said the one called Perdita, with a note of vicious triumph. "Told you so, Emma. No matter how pretty and perfect it all seems. Sooner or later, the rent comes due."

~

The second marriage of the Earl of Sandwich could only be described as a scandal. His first marriage was the opposite of that.

His original Countess, Ana Margareta, was a solid, practical sort of woman: easily bored, always busy and quick to judge. She appeared in all her portraits as if she were a great deal prettier, paler and kinder of spirit than the sturdy, practical mother Liesl remembered.

Portrait painters only believed in one type of dead

mother: a wan and ethereal creature, perfectly-mannered, and discreetly fading out of memory.

The Earl and the first Countess were not quite cousins, but their families were close enough that their marriage had been a foregone conclusion from the time they born.

Liesl's mother preferred gardening to formal parties. She was never happier than when wearing a thick striped apron, armed with a pair of secateurs for dead-heading the roses. She taught all of her daughters everything they needed to know about running a successful household, and outsourced the skills she had no interest in — dancing, curtseying, terms of address, basic magic — to boarding schools and a series of specialised tutors. She spent her entire marriage fighting a war of sarcasm and one-upman-ship with her mother-in-law the Dowager Countess, and only out-lived that particularly sour old lady by a single year.

FROM: *LADY LIESL OF SANDWICH, APHRODITE VILLA, BRIGHTSIDE, THE ISLE OF BATH)*

TO: *ANA-MARGARETA DANVILLE BATTENBURG-SEVILLE, FORMER COUNTESS OF SANDWICH, (DECEASED)*

Dearest Mamma,

The aunties and cousins waited six months after your demise to plan his next marriage. They agonised over a 'suitable candidate' who could 'provide those poor mites with a mother.'

It was too late. Before they could even refine their shortlist, the Earl confounded the lot of them. He dropped his old friends, ran wild with poets, and finally eloped with Miss Emma Lamb, an entirely unsuitable daughter of no-one-was-quite-sure with a chequered past as an actress and artist's model.

Here's my confession: I've never hated Emma. Even if Anna and Retta are correct to suspect she was his mistress before you ever left us, I hold no grudge.

Even if she's the same age as Gustav (barely twenty-eight!).

Even if she stole our father and transformed him into an utterly unfamiliar creature.

~~Even if their scandal ruined my chances of a good marriage.~~

That part's not fair. The Great Sandwich Scandal had faded by the time I came Out. When an Earl falls from grace, Society bends over backwards to re-classify him him as eccentric. My three elder sisters were all married and settled in respectable households, and they blame Father and Emma for ruining my chances to do the same.

I'm an adult woman and I ruined my chances all on my own.

No, I've never begrudged the Earl and his new Countess their happiness.

Except of course, that they're no longer happy. Clearly, something has gone terribly wrong. And for some reason, my father thinks that I can fix it.

Look at me, playing matchmaker and detective. Would you be proud of me, or would you be more interested in hearing which root vegetables were planted in the kitchen garden at Battenburg Abbey this year?

Parsnips. It's parsnips.

Your aching, half orphaned daughter,
Liesl.

❧

"*L*et me introduce everyone," Emma said, for all the world as if she had nothing to hide. "You've met Perdita."

"Charmed," said the indecently-draped woman, watching Liesl like a cat ready to pounce on a stray herring.

"Perdita Cholmondley, that is," Emma went on. "She's a marvellous fresco painter, and sculptor. First woman to be admitted to the Pygmalion Academy."

"First woman to be kicked out of the Pygmalion Academy,"drawled the shabby man with the beard.

"And this is Meredith Merryweather."

"The Poet King," the shabby man corrected, offering a surprisingly genteel hand to Liesl.

"No one's going to call you that, Merry," sighed Emma.

"Don't shatter my dreams, Emma."

"This one is the *terribly famous* Basil Robucks. Art critic and fashion icon. He used to dabble in painting, but these days he prefers to make other painters weep into their beautifully tailored sleeves." There was a lilt of humour in her voice with this particular introduction.

This one, Liesl had heard of. "You gave a lecture at my sister's school," she informed Mr Robucks politely.

"I did?" The young man didn't look old enough to give a lecture on anything. He was beautifully garbed in layers of iris-on-violet, which made his pale skin look rather sickly. His hair was jet black, and flopped in his face in a manner that was either entirely out of fashion, or about to be the next big thing in male fringes. "That doesn't sound like me."

"It started out as a lecture on the most celebrated portrait painters of the last century, and ended up being about how to spot which gentlemen one should avoid at balls, based on how they tie their cravat." Liesl could not help a tiny twitch of a smile. "Clytie assured me it was the most useful education she had ever received in a single hour."

"Yes," said Basil thoughtfully, tapping his chin. "That sounds *more* like me."

"And this is Indigo Larkin," Emma finished, gesturing to the young girl at her feet. "Model, muse and dear companion."

Indigo looked rather startlingly like Emma — she wore her hair in the same careless style, though the shade and curl looked rather more deliberate, as if she was attempting to copy the Countess. Her dress was near-identical, too — dusky rose instead of blue, but the same cut, even down to the paint daubs on the bodice and hem.

Indigo was the least friendly of the bunch, not even pretending to smile at Liesl in greeting. "George's daughters never come here," she said in chilly tones.

Liesl had felt unmoored through this entire scene, and yet this was the most surprising moment: she so rarely heard her father's first name on anyone's lips. He was 'Earl' or 'Sandwich' to his peers and his mother, 'My Lord' to the servants. Liesl's mamma had always called him 'Bats,' shortening the family name of Battenburg-Seville with her usual dry wit.

George. Who was this girl, barely Liesl's age, to call him that?

There was a pause, awkward enough that it demanded to be filled.

"And yet," Liesl said a beat too late, smiling with a sweetness she often called upon in company. It was her usual armour against cruel wit and open curiosity about her family. "Here I am."

Another awkward pause commenced, and this time she felt no obligation to fill it.

3

THE FAMILY JEWELS

"*D*on't mind them," Emma said in a cheerful tone as she swept Liesl upstairs to the private family floor. "They're not used to mixing with the gentry."

"You're a Countess," Liesl said, a little tartly. "Besides, aren't they also my father's friends?"

"He doesn't act the Earl around them," said Emma with a shrug, as if titles could be put on and off at will, saved for Sunday best. "As for me, well. I barely count at the best of times. The Countess who didn't count, ha!"

"You shouldn't say that where anyone might hear," said Liesl, a little shocked.

Emma did not look the least concerned. "You're not anyone, my dear. You're family."

~

*T*here was no sign of Amie, and no clue as to which rooms had been assigned to Liesl and her maid. Instead, Emma led her into a lavish dressing room, and then through the glass doors to a covered balcony. From here you could see over the edge of a cliff to a view that was all sea and sky, though there was little light left in either of them. A few gaslamp beacons flickering here and there along the cliff path illuminated what must be a glorious vision in daylight.

It was not warm. Emma passed a thick woollen wrap to Liesl and then layered another over the shawl she already wore.

"The servants think I'm mad for spending so much time out here," she said. "But I can't get enough of that sea air. I know every island has a coast, but there's something special about the Isle of Bath. I feel better just for breathing it in."

"Must be because everyone here is on holiday," said Liesl, more snarky than she had intended.

Emma gave her a startled look and then burst into laughter. "I knew I'd like you," she said. "George seemed so certain we would loathe each other."

I wouldn't worry about it, Liesl thought. *Anna, Retta and Gerda loathe you enough for all of us.*

"He sent me, you know," she said before Emma got any ideas about Liesl being here out of the kindness of her heart.

"Oh, I know that," said Emma. She took a deep break of the cooling night air, sea salt and all. "Go on, then, Rip off the bandage. What does the Earl wish of his wayward wife?"

Liesl took a deep breath, resenting her father for making her do this; for making her be the one to bring the message. Gustav would probably have enjoyed being the one to put the boot in. Anna would have sold tickets.

She had felt important to be asked; now, faced with the

sweet and open face of her stepmother, she felt quite sick to her stomach.

"He wanted me to tell you that he knows about the diamond," she admitted with a sigh. "And he's very cross about it." Livid, was a more accurate description.

Emma blinked, several times. "What diamond?"

~

The Battenburg-Seville family were in the privileged position of needing to request clarification when a question arose about diamonds. There were several obvious potential culprits:

1) the large and glittering radiant-cut betrothal ring that technically belonged to Emma, as it had to the previous eleven Countesses of Sandwich. Her betrothal was so short that she had never had a chance to wear it in public. As a family jewel the ring would be passed on to Gustav's intended, but there was no rush. At five-and-twenty, no one was pressing a Viscount to make his match. Meanwhile, his sisters would be considered old maids if any of them reached that age unwed. Two of Liesl's three elder sisters had worn the family ring for their betrothals, before swapping it out for something more modern and delicate in a wedding band. Gerda, whose betrothal came shortly after they all acquired a new stepmother, flat-out refused to ask for it.

2) a solid, rather old-fashioned tiara, worn by all Seville ladies upon their first ball, and their weddings, for twelve generations. Roughly the same size and shape as the box it came in, and about as comfortable to wear.

3) the Prima-donna Diamond, a gratuitously expensive necklace which the Earl had infamously purchased off the neck of an opera singer and presented to Emma on their

first anniversary, while holidaying on the Continent. It was a large diamond teardrop set with twelve amethysts, and a further twenty-four tiny pink sapphires, in white gold. Tasteless, gaudy, and every bit as extravagant as Aphrodite Villa.

Further evidence that this marriage would be the ruin of their family, according to Anna, Retta, Gerda and occasionally, Gustav.

~

"Oh, that thing," said Emma, rolling her eyes. "I might have known George would be more concerned with baubles than his wife. I'm surprised you've taken on the job of ferrying love tokens back and forth, Liesl. Don't you have another Season to prepare for?"

That was a sore subject, and not one Liesl was prepared to discuss with a near stranger. "He *knows*," she said heavily. "The diamond was sold in Town two weeks ago, Countess. Did you think he wouldn't find out?"

There must worse ways to discover that one's estranged spouse was planning a divorce, but learning she was secretly selling off the family jewels was quite high on the list.

"The Prima-donna Diamond…" Emma looked genuinely shocked. "*No.*"

"It's not a difficult necklace to identify," Liesl said, a little unsettled. She had not known what to expect from this conversation, but certainly not surprise on the part of her stepmother.

Emma hurried back through her dressing room and into the bedchamber beyond. Which was… well, there they were again with words like 'gaudy' and 'extravagant' running through Liesl's head in a voice that sounded

remarkably like that of her dead grandmamma, the
Dowager Countess. The room featured an enormous bed,
draped in red and purple like something out of a Royal
suite. Gilt and paintings everywhere, though the paintings
were a great deal more modern than the furnishings.
Indeed, one giant canvas featured a lithe young woman
covered only in a few discreetly placed posies of flowers…
oh, it was a portrait of Emma.

The portrait, enchanted as so many were these days,
dropped her stepdaughter a lascivious wink and did a slight
shimmy, allowing some crucial petals to fall.

Liesl found herself blushing and looking away, but
luckily the painting had no further antics to inflict upon
her. Emma was too busy to notice. She fussed with an
antique dressing table, fishing out an ornate lockbox, which
she opened with a key from her charm bracelet. A whispered word (used several times times, with increasing impa-
tience and frustration) enlarged the charm to match the
lock… and behold, the box was empty.

"Neptune's salty balls," Emma exclaimed. "I swear, I
didn't sell it. I wouldn't. I love that damned necklace, shiny
monstrosity that it is. Does George really think I sold it?"
She sounded honest, her voice tinged with panic. But of
course, she was an actress.

"Are you saying it was stolen?" Liesl did her best to not
sound dubious.

Emma's eyes narrowed. "Let me guess. Your father is in
a strop because he believes I'm selling off the family jewels
as part of some kind of escape plan. Honestly, what a
goose he is. When I want a divorce, he'll know about it."

"I believe you," said Liesl. "But I'm not sure my father
will." The Earl was been furious when she last saw him,
storming up and down the corridors of the family manor.

"Shit." Emma looked devastated. "I came here for —

21

well, for a good reason. I needed to get a breath of fresh air and give him a chance to fix what is between us. It's been so lovely, chatting with my friends, making art — I've been painting for the first time in years. Something about being here is just so inspiring. I feel like myself again. If he thinks I've sold off the greatest love token he ever bought me, he'll never take me back. His pride won't let him."

Liesl was already thinking ahead. "Are you the only one with a key to that box?"

"George has one, I think, tossed in with all his household keys, four islands from here." Emma held a hand to her forehead like a headache was coming. "It can't be the servants, either. Only Torquay the butler and Tavistock the maid of all work have access to this floor, and they're both cursed."

Liesl wasn't sure if she had heard right. "Cursed?"

"To ensure loyalty to the household," said Emma, a frown creasing her forehead. "The Earl insisted we follow tradition when Aphrodite Villa was built, especially as those two would be managing the property for many months of the year when the rest of them are not in residence. The curse prevents them from stealing from us, or telling any secrets outside the…" she trailed off, looking even more upset. "Is that not a family tradition?"

"It's barbaric!" Liesl explained. "No one in the old families curses their servants any more. Even Grandmamma stopped doing it eventually, and she was the worst snob imaginable!"

She did, of course, punctuate every holiday meal with a rant about how standards had slipped since society stopped cursing servants, but Emma didn't need to know that detail right that minute.

The Countess threw up her hands. "How was I to

know? I married into this aristocratic bullshit, you can't expect me to know what's normal for you lot."

"Maybe if you made an effort to make friends with our sort of people instead of those wild creatures downstairs, you wouldn't make such errors," Liesl snapped, and then instantly regretted it. *Our sort of people?* She sounded exactly like Grandmamma.

Emma gave her a dirty look. "Those wild creatures as you call them, are some of my dearest, closest… oh gods, it has to be one of them, doesn't it?"

Obviously, though Liesl was glad she hadn't had to suggest it first. "Did any of your friends know about the necklace? What it looked like, where it was kept?"

"All of them," Emma said miserably. "We performed an opera over supper a few weeks ago. I wore the necklace for that, and Tavistock brought me the box in front of all of them."

"Just these four house guests?"

"Just these four my favourite people in the world, yes." Emma looked sick.

Liesl sighed. "Unless you've spent intimate time with anyone else recently — intimate enough to get that key off your bracelet and unlock the box, then return the charm…"

"The box is cursed too," Emma said miserably. "If anyone tries to open it without the key, it screams 'property of the Countess of Sandwich' at a very unpleasant pitch."

"Oh, I had one of those," Liesl said sympathetically. "It said 'property of Lady Liesl' plus all eight of my middle names. When I was six I jammed a spoon in the keyhole and eventually Father made the footmen bury it under the croquet lawn to shut the thing up."

"You have to help me," said Emma, seizing her hand.

"Liesl, please. These are my friends. I can't accuse them of anything until I know for certain which has done it."

"Me?" More surprises. "What do you expect me to do?"

"Your father must be shown proof it wasn't me. He probably has a horde of solicitors drawing up divorce papers as we speak. You're my last hope to keep this marriage in one piece." An arch expression crossed Emma's face. "Unless you want me out of this family…"

"Oh don't you dare," Liesl said crossly. "I'm not my siblings. I've given you a fair shot, haven't it?"

"You have!" Emma insisted, clutching both hands now. "That's why you're the only person I can trust."

"To solve the mystery of the Prima-donna Diamond?" Liesl bit her lip. Solving a mystery was hardly her cup of tea. She definitely remembered deciding not to do any such thing when she first arrived at this outrageously beautiful villa.

"Please, Liesl. Say yes? You're my only hope."

~

*F*rom: *Lady Liesl of Sandwich, Aphrodite Villa, Brightside, the Isle of Bath)*

To: *Lady Margery Foulkkes-Hobb, Viscountess Dudley, Mallow Manor, Isle of Glass*

Dearest Margery

Thank you so much for forwarding your latest novel to me, the one about the blacksmith's daughter and the Count of Nemesis.

Not the real Count of Nemesis, of course, but the gloomy magister prince that you loosely based on the Count of Nemesis. How subtle you are to change his hair colour and preferred dog breed in order to retain deniability. No one shall ever guess the truth.

It seems as if every girl we went to school with is writing novels these days, ~~or at least those of you who married in your first Season, as if to remind me how out of sync I have become with you all.~~ Every other postal packet arrives with tales of gloomy houses on hills, plucky young women being bricked up in priest-holes, sinister butlers, murderous maids, and the surprising betrayals of dearly beloved family members. I can't think how any of you you find the time.

~~Even with the occasional plot-twist of a wife or a were-wolf in the attic, these books all carry a tone suggesting you are happier in your marriages than my older sisters, whose 'friends' still write novels exposing each other's affairs with other friends' husbands…~~

Do you remember what I was like at school? That first year, I mean, before I learned that my natural reserve was being interpreted as cold and stuck-up to the other girls. Then later, when I thought the only way to make friends was to let them treat me like a doormat.

You were such a help, Margery. You taught me how to act agreeably, how to offer shoulders to cry on and a pocket money purse to borrow from. You taught me to share my cakes, and somehow you always ended up with the largest slice.

My, you enjoyed teaching me things.

In truth, the whole business made me feel terrible about myself. I thought the only way to keep any of you as my friends was to say 'yes, how can I help?' every time I was asked for a favour.

I'm not quite the girl I was at school. For all my failures in the marriage market, I've grown some confidence along the way, and a spine to go with it. I've gained friends who enjoy it when I speak my mind. I've bribed officials and stayed out late at parties. I've become just a little — dare I say it — rebellious.

And yet, faced with a large pair of blue eyes and a wobbling lower lip, it's so easy to fall back into old patterns. Good old Liesl. You can count on her.

I could blame many people for my natural compliance. My horrid grandmamma, my busy mamma, my distant father. My sisters, never quite bothering to listen to a word I say, too busy squawking at each other. My brother, who doesn't even pretend to be interested. The world, telling me that being pretty and witty and rich and eligible isn't enough — anything short of perfection is failure.

But today I'm blaming you, because you wrote a novel about a plucky young lady in an unfamiliar house who traps a jewel thief, solves three murders, and marries a Count at the end (even if he turns out to be a werewolf).

I read it all the way to the end, and I'm rather afraid that it inspired some terrible life decisions.

Odd thing, inspiration. You never quite know where it's going to strike.

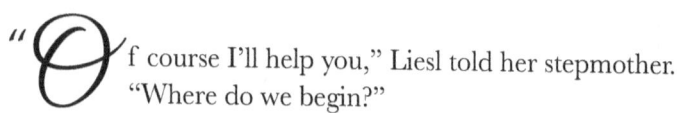

"Of course I'll help you," Liesl told her stepmother. "Where do we begin?"

4

BREAKFAST IN BOHEMIA

"Obviously I'll help you," announced Amie, once she and Liesl had found each other again, in a bedroom on the guest (not the family) floor. She was recovered from her travel-sickness, which came as a great relief to them both.

"Help with what?" Liesl asked, her thoughts still on Emma.

"Your investigation," said Amie, reaching for the hairbrush. "You can't do it alone, miss."

Liesl stared at her in the mirror. "What do you have in mind?"

"There's more eyes and ears in this house than the Countess and her fancy guests in their funny clothes," the maid huffed. "You need *me* to talk to everyone else."

Of course she did. Liesl should have thought of that herself.

The truth was, she assumed she could trace the necklace and its thief fairly easily. Scrying had always been one of her better magical skills, along with sympathetic magic. She had, however, spent half an hour gazing into the washing basin, attempting to call up the face of the one who had stolen Emma's necklace, and hadn't produced so much as a shadow.

It wasn't that magic didn't work around here. She felt quite normal, and had managed a few minor spells. But there was less strength than usual to every enchantment she managed to achieve, as if there was something else sapping all natural magic out of the general are.

It made her feel tired and terribly vulnerable. It also meant that she could not rely on all her usual resources to solve this particular problem.

Thus, Amie's offer of assistance was something for which to be really rather grateful.

"I absolutely need your help," Liesl told her. "What do you know so far?"

"I've had a good poke around downstairs already," said Amie, giving Liesl's hair a good tug and freeing all the tiny braids from their snood. "There's barely a handful of staff, less'n you'd think for a house this big. They must use a tonne of cleaning charms every month."

"Yes," said Liesl dubiously. Domestic magic was one of the skills her tutors had been especially firm that she learn, if only so she could tell when her servants were doing it wrong. She was as certain as she could be that Aphrodite Villa did not use cleaning charms at all — or if they did, it must be a bewilderingly extravagant form of charm that left no magical trace in the air.

"There's the butler Mr Torquay and the maid-of-all-work Miss Tavistock," Amie went on. "She fancies herself housekeeper but no one calls her that and it's not like she has more than one maid under her. And the butler, what a character! He's never around when you want him, not like every butler in every house I've ever been in. But he has a pencil moustache and he wears a top hat everywhere, if you can believe it. A top hat! Who ever heard of such a thing in a butler."

"A most unusual household," Liesl agreed. "Who else?"

"There's the cook, Mrs Pennance. She has a Past and no mistake. I heard Bets the tweeny gossiping with Bert the stable lad, and they said she's from Town originally, the Countess brought her from the theatre."

The latter was said with a little sigh, as if coming from the theatre was something romantic and not a decidedly odd reference for a cook.

"She travels wherever the Countess goes," Amie went on. "So Torquay and Tavistock must do for themselves when there's no master or mistress here."

"And what else?" asked Liesl.

"What indeed!" said Amie indignantly. "There's nothing else! No scullery maids, parlour maids, chamber maids, no footman except when his Lordship's in residence and *he* brings his own. They can't keep extra staff because of all the rumours about this house and those — disreputable guests." She said the last in something of a loud whisper. "Who don't have staff themselves, not one maid for either of those ladies. Only Mr Robucks has a valet: Evans. My, doesn't that young man think he's the cat's pyjamas, wearing his master's cast-offs. Honestly, I'm surprised the butler is still here himself, he has such dreadful mutterings to say about her Ladyship's friends."

"Mr Torquay is cursed," Liesl said calmly. "Miss Tavistock, too. Loyalty to the house. The old oath."

Amie sucked in a breath. "That happened to my grandmam when she was a girl. I didn't think lords did that no more."

"They don't," Liesl said firmly. "But my father was raised in a rather old-fashioned household. I suppose some of it must have stuck." Her mamma and strong pragmatic streak must have been the only reason they didn't curse servants at Battenburg Abbey when Liesl was a child, which was a very uncomfortable sort of thought. "The necklace went missing from a charmed box in the Countess's chamber," she said aloud. "She said no servants have access to the family floor except Torquay and Tavistock, does that sounds right to you?"

"Oh, yes," said Amie firmly. "They made such a song and dance about Bets the tweeny never going above the dining room, and gave me such a stare when I told them I must have access to your room. I think that's why they put you down here with the guests and not on the family floor with her Ladyship. What do they think a maid is for?"

"Perhaps they don't want you to be corrupted by the more personal artwork," Liesl said lightly.

"Too late for that, miss, I've seen the fresco in the downstairs lavatory." Amie clicked her tongue. "Only time I've ever worked in a household with those sorts of rules about forbidden floors, is when they don't trust the gentlemen…" She stopped, stricken.

"Don't trust the gentlemen?" Liesl repeated.

"To keep their hands to themselves," Amie whispered, embarrassed.

Liesl had not thought that of her father. Even after his choice of new bride and his wild Bohemian ways, she had never considered… "I'm sure it's just because of the art, and to protect the Countess' reputation from that of her guests," she said. "Especially if the Villa has had trouble keeping staff."

"Can I do more?" Amie said. "Please, miss. I can help."

"I know you can," said Liesl. "Be discreet, but… I do need to know if any of the Countess' guests — or any of the servants other than Torquay and Tavistock — left the island, or went anywhere on their own to meet someone in the last few weeks. Since the opera that my stepmother performed for her guests. Somehow, the necklace was smuggled out of this house and sold in Town."

"By portal?" Amie said dubiously.

"I'm assuming they didn't travel by swan-shaped boat!"

Her maid had a good point. There were no convenient portals nearby. Hopefully that would make it easier to discover who had made the journey by train and curricle and thus, who had taken the Prima-donna Diamond, without further need for Liesl to make a spectacle of herself in the asking of awkward questions.

Or to strain her already-limited magic beyond its apparent limits.

～

FROM: *LADY LIESL BATTENBURG-SEVILLE OF SANDWICH, APHRODITE VILLA, BRIGHTSIDE, THE ISLE OF BATH*

TO: *LADY CLYTIE BATTENBURG-SEVILLE OF SANDWICH, THE NAISMITH NESBIT SCHOOL FOR GIRLS, THE ISLE OF THYME*

Dearest Clytie

I hope you're having a wondrous time at school, and that you received the parcel of jam and cakes I sent from Town before I set off on my travels.

You'll be Out yourself soon enough, so I thought I'd share some sisterly wisdom on the social situations in which you may be flung.

House parties.

They seem like they should be more relaxed than balls or assemblies, but they're so much worse because you need to be on display at all times, showing off your skills as a potential wife. The gracious hostess, the charming conversationalist.

At breakfast, for instance, you can't just drag yourself to the table in a sloppy robe and throw kedgeree at your face like you do at home. You must be careful and awake. You smile and make unthreatening, self-deprecating remarks. You agree to any activity that sounds even slightly merry, in order to be known as a good sport. You also find a reason to compliment every other lady at least once a day, especially if she's been a beast to you.

Don't starve yourself; better to eat generous portions, so no one else feels self-conscious about nibbling on toast in front of gentlemen. A touch of sympathetic magic does not hurt here and there, to soften hearts and warm everyone towards you.

(Don't overdo the latter when in pursuit of another person, whether friend or suitor. I'm a little ashamed of how blatantly I have used magic in such situations. Less is more.)

I'm sure you are not used to devoting so much effort to being liked, but this is the key currency of an unmarried young lady of quality. If the whole party like you, they will be on your side and wish you well. If they hate you, then it does not matter how much a gentleman admires you, he will never cross his friends to take your hand.

This applies, of course to a normal house party, one with the proper number of eligible unmarrieds and their chaperones. One where the agenda is open and clear.

I'm currently staying in a house with a very different assortment of guests. There's simply no one here to marry, and no one to befriend in manner that might prove useful in the future.

All our grandmamma's greatest fears have come to pass: I am lost in Bohemia. I'm not sure if she ever knew if this was a fictional or real place, but she certainly had opinions about the creatures who resided there: the poets and artists and muses and laudanum-drinkers.

I do not know how to make such people like me. How can I possibly talk to them without sounding like… well, like Grandmamma?

<u>Brave heart</u>, *Liesl*, our mamma might have said. Though in truth, she was more likely to say <u>Wipe your nose, Liesl, and don't track that mud into the house. The maids have enough to do</u>.

Dead mothers are most unhelpful, don't you find?

Let me know what colour ribbons you want me to send you for half-term. Or do you need a new bonnet? Don't let Gerda buy one for you, her tastes have gone quite bizarre since she discovered yellow sateen.

Your loving sister,
Liesl

❧

*L*iesl dressed in her simplest day dress, a white muslin appropriate for summer (assuming the sun came out over Brightside today). She threw a light lavender shawl over it, which had a few 'be your best self' charms woven into the edges, for confidence. Amie, excited to begin her own day of detective work, dressed Liesl's hair in a simple, elegant style.

She could do this. It was only breakfast.

Except, of course, it was breakfast *and catching a jewel thief*.

In daylight, Aphrodite Villa was even more extravagantly glamorous than the night before. All the white marble and bright tiles in the foyer gleamed like they had been cleaned by pixies overnight.

(Was this Miss Tavistock's work, or that of the hard-working tweeny?)

The breakfast room faced the ocean. It featured wide glass doors showing a bright blue sky and seagulls circling overhead, beyond a lovely green curve of a garden. It was also empty of guests; Bohemians, it seemed, were late risers and yet to touch the silver dishes of breakfast food, which must have recently served up because they were piping hot, but unusually for a house this size, not covered in preservation charms.

The walls of the breakfast room were covered in a sensuous mural of nymphs and dryads at play, thankfully covered with rather more in the way of artful drapery than the portraits that were to be found in the bedrooms. (Liesl had not yet dared to examine the fresco in the downstairs lavatory.)

Here at least there was a sign of magic, though the nymphs and dryads were not properly enchanted to run about in a wild manner, as was the fashion for such artwork these days — no, it was more clever than that. They seemed *almost* to move. As her eyes were drawn across the mural, Liesl felt the winsome creatures giggling to themselves and dancing in the corner of her eye, though when she looked properly they were but paint on a wall.

"My best work, I think," said a dry voice.

Liesl jumped; there had been no one in the room, and now Perdita Cholmondley, she of the feline eyes and sensuous drapery, was sitting at the table with a cup of tea in front of her.

34

"I didn't —" said Liesl, and then stopped. "You weren't there a moment ago."

The artist raised a lazy shoulder — she was dressed in men's pyjamas, striped from collar to ankle. Ironically, though some might consider it scandalous to wear night clothes to the breakfast table, she was more thoroughly clad than she had been the night before. "I don't enjoy chatter at breakfast. Invisibility is a useful trick for ignoring dull companions."

"You're talking to me," Liesl observed.

Perdita smiled warmly. Her dark hair fell about her shoulders in an effortless way. It was as if she truly did not care what she looked like; and thus, looked magnificent. "I don't find you dull."

Liesl busied herself about a cup of tea for herself, and a plate of buttered muffin. She could not quite face baked eggs or fish so early in the morning.

She sat near Perdita, when she came to the table; the artist preened as if she had won something.

"Did you really paint all this?" Liesl asked.

"I enjoy murals," said Perdita, over the brim of her cup. "Portraiture is such a bore these days, with everyone so determined you capture their loved one and the family Pekinese in such exact detail. Who can be bothered? There's more freedom in a mural. One can really breathe and play."

Out of the corner of her eye, Liesl was sure the nymphs and dryads were playing too; nudging each other and throwing their heads back in laughter. "I stayed at a house once where the parlour had enchanted kittens painted on the walls," she said. "They constantly chased each other back and forth, back and forth. It was exhausting. I like yours better."

Compliment each lady at least once a day.

"Mmm," said Perdita. "So do I. Though I'll confess it wasn't intentional. It's an odd house for magic. Spells seem to end up with the most peculiar effects, or no effect at all. I can make myself as invisible as I choose, but can I make a dryad flash her nether regions at passing guests? Apparently not!"

That at least explained why basic household spells for cleaning and keeping food hot were not applied here... though it did not explain who was doing all the extra work.

Did the butler do everything? And if so, why had Liesl not yet set eyes upon him? Butlers did not usually hide in sculleries.

"You're a painter *and* a sculptor?" Liesl pressed. She was not quite sure how one discovered if one of their fellow guests was a potential jewel thief or not, so she had determined just to keep asking questions until something shook loose. She would try some minor divination later, possibly outside of the grounds

"So I am. But there's no money in granite, and I can rarely afford marble — one can't pay the bills by selling a piece every few years. One has to get creative." Perdita had all manner of smiles; this one showed all her teeth, some of which were rather pointed. "I've offended you. Toffs don't like to talk about money much, I hear?"

"Only when we're spending it," Liesl said lightly.

That, at least, made the artist laugh. "As long as you're spending it on art, who am I to complain?"

It took another cup of tea and a second plate of buttered muffins before Liesl felt confident to inquire about the other members of the house party. *You're investigating, so investigate!*

"The Countess and I don't know each other very well," she began. "And I'm afraid I'm desperately out of touch with the art scene. I've never heard of most of her friends."

"Your father's friends too," said Perdita, surprisingly. "At least, when he's not being a knob."

"So not very often, then." Liesl hadn't meant to say that, but it made Perdita laugh again, which was reward in itself. "Is Mr Merryweather really a famous poet?" she tried.

"Clearly not, if you've never heard of him." Perdita sighed with her whole body, her curves barely held in check by the sturdy men's pyjamas. "He won one poetry contest a few years ago, and never quite recovered from it, poor soul. He's convinced he's the next great thing, but I don't think he's written a line all year."

"He doesn't seem to have packed for a house party," Liesl tried tact. The man was clothed like a peasant from last century.

"Oh, that's just to annoy Basil. He thinks he's such an expert on men's fashion — of course, he is, which makes it worse. Merry got sick of being criticised every time he selected a cravat, so he swore to wear nothing but sackcloth and ashes in Basil's presence from now on. At least, I think that's why it started. He wears those dreadful clothes every-where now. I swear he got it into his head that it's more artistic to look like you just rolled out of a hay barn."

"And Miss Larkin?" Liesl went on. "How long has she known you all?"

It was one question too many. Perdita put her teacup down. "You're a curious creature, aren't you?"

"Just finding my feet," Liesl said, with a light laugh she often used to diffuse tensions. It didn't work.

"Why exactly do you need to know all the details about our friends?" Perdita went on, those cat's eyes of hers narrowed "Reporting back to the Earl are you? All our scandalous doings. You can't tell him anything about us he doesn't know for himself. Georgie-porgie was happy enough to run in our circles and laugh at our jokes before he had this latest quarrel with his wife."

"I'm not spying for my father," said Liesl, surprised at the thought. "I'm on Emma's side."

"Taking sides? So there *is* a disagreement." Perdita had turned quite savage. "What do you know?"

Liesl threw up her hands. "Nothing, I know nothing. You flummox me," she added crossly.

That, oddly enough, seemed to calm Perdita. "I do have that effect on people," she agreed, sounding pleased.

"Are we late? Where's the bacon?" Basil Robucks, dressed immaculately in tailored black with only a hint of emerald green at his cuffs, strolled into the breakfast room and made for the covered salvers. "Perdita, my duck! Not invisible this morning?"

"I am discovered," said Perdita.

"And our new guest! What fun." Basil began piling up a plate with an exorbitant pile of food: eggs and fish and bacon and muffins all teetering in a stack. "Tell me, Miss Humptlety-Whatsit, what do you do?"

"What do I do?" Liesl repeated. It was not a question generally asked of ladies of quality, who were generally expected to be, rather than do.

Basil sat at the table opposite her, plunking down his laden plate and an over-filled up of coffee. He then tucked an enormous linen napkin around himself, to protect his precious clothes. "Your medium of choice, my dear. Oils, or watercolours? Clay or basket-weaving? Do you write poetry, or those long gossipy novels that are all the rage?" He looked slightly aghast. "You're not a musician, are you?"

"Basil, darling," said Perdita. "Have you considered that she may not be an artist at all?"

He gaped at them both, mouth working like a fish out of water; it was an act, quite clearly. No one could be that much of a chump. And yet, he got away with his performance by being stupidly charming. "How would that work?" he asked finally.

Liesl laughed; a genuine laugh, not the false one she had practiced so expertly for so long. "My art," she said. "Is to select the right gowns for balls and parties, and promenade around, making friends and being both charming and delightful, in the hope of catching the right sort of husband."

Basil made a show of considering this, as if he had never heard of Society before. "And are you any good at this art of yours?" he asked.

"No," said Liesl, startling herself. One never admitted such things in public. "I thought I was, but the results speak for themselves. Two Seasons, no husband. I'm an utter failure."

Perdita snorted.

Basil forked some bacon into his mouth, and chewed furiously. "It's never too late, my dear," he said a moment later, dabbing his face with a napkin. "You might like to *try* watercolours."

5

A MOST SURPRISING PROMENADE

TO: *THE LATE, FORMER DOWAGER COUNTESS OF SANDWICH, GERDRUTTE TALBOY BATTENBURG-SEVILLE OF SANDWICH (DECEASED)*

FROM: *THE VERY MUCH ALIVE, MUCH YOUNGER, DEEPLY INFURIATED LADY LIESL BATTENBURG-SEVILLE OF SANDWICH*

*D*ear Grandmamma
I blame you.
How were we, the many daughters of the Earl of Sandwich, expected to grow up with anything other than an expectation of absolute perfection, with you glaring at us from every corner through your ivory-rimmed monocle?
I still can't walk down a staircase without the memory of your crab-claw hands grabbing me through the banisters while you shrieked "Stand up straight!"

(Grandmamma, I always stand up straight. I was terrified to do otherwise.)

I don't believe I ever wished you dead. But I recall at your funeral feeling such a dizzying sense of relief that you would not be there to comment on my first Season.

Not that I would have disgraced you.

I excelled. I was a credit to my family. I have, as it turns out, a talent for charming people, letting them think that I think they're marvellous. I dance well, I converse brilliantly. I can snap open a fan with a flick of my wrist, like I've been doing it my whole life.

(Tuition in this particular skill did in fact begin when I was three years old.)

But excellence was not enough for me, not with my childhood. Not the ghost of your standards embossed into my spine. I was rolled paper-thin and stamped hard with the determination to be perfect.

I know you had plenty to say about my older sisters' choices at the time, but they did rather well in the marriage mart: between them they caught a country Baronet, a Lord, and a wealthy banker on his way to at least an honorary Honorable.

I planned to better them all. During my first Season, I smiled and flattered and spoke in a soft, amused voice. I used every magical and social trick in the book. I called in all debts of friendship, got invited to the most fashionable balls… and in the final act, with several potential suitors on the line, I threw all my coin on a single roll of the dice. An exclusive house party, with the chance to marry a Duke.

You would have approved, except for the part where I failed.

Many noblewomen of fine families emerge from their first Season without an engagement, or even a formal understanding. It's nothing to be ashamed of. Other grand-mammas would not have bullied Retta mercilessly for not bringing her Lord up to scratch until halfway through her second Season.

Even two Seasons without a betrothal is not a disas-trous outcome, according to the standards of anyone who is not you, Grandmamma. Three is the number after which a respectable young lady begins to be gently pitied by her peers.

I hate that I can still hear your voice in my head. I hate that your voice got louder after the Great Duke Failure. It wasn't as if, at the end, I even wanted to marry Henry. He's far better matched with Juno, and I'm thankful that he — beautiful dolt that he is — had the wit to realise that before it was too late.

And yet.

That voice in my head, the one that sounds exactly like you, keeps telling me how disappointing it is that I did not end up the Duchess of Storm.

The truth is — and you would despise me for this — I didn't even try, after that. I spent half of my second Season out of Town, and the rest ignoring all the eligible suitors. And I learned something astounding. The parties are more enjoyable, the suppers more delectable, and the friendships far more warm and genuine when you're not spending all your earthly energies trying to catch a husband.

Perfection is exhausting. I was due a little fun. I have no regrets.

~~After less than a day of being flirted at by Perdita Chol-mondley it's starting to occur to me that I may not even be all that attracted to men. They may wear suits nicely, but not one of my dance partners ever made my stomach swoop quite so much as she does with those eyes and that smile and…~~

And yet it hurt, to fail.

I've never failed at anything before.

There you are, inside my head, reminding me of that failure along with all the other tiny imperfections of my life thus far.

I don't want a third Season. I don't want any of it. I am terrified of becoming a joke, that terribly eligible, terribly pretty, terribly charming Lady Liesl who can't catch a husband, what must be wrong with her?

I'm frightened to try.

(I'm frightened to admit I don't want to try anymore.)

(What even is there for me, if I'm not hunting a Husband of Quality? What would my life look like?)

I'm frightened that the crabby, screechy, awfully cold voice that lives inside my head — the one that sounds so much like you — is all that's stopping me from running away and leaving everything behind.

(Not you, though, Grandmamma. I'll never be rid of you.)

Your devoted, battered, somehow steadfast grand-daughter,

Liesl

❦

*A*fter escaping Perdita and Basil, whose banter had descended into a kind of mutual self-mockery that left her feeling more of an outsider than ever, Liesl took a little time to herself, writing letters in the Aphrodite Villa library, a white-pillared beast of a room better suited for sculptures on plinths than books on the wall.

(It had both, including a startling marble bust of Liesl's own father, almost unrecognisable with his mouth distorted in laughter. Artist: Miss P Cholmondley.)

Too many letters. She began with a short note to a friend, and they somehow built up, the words spilling over. She was writing to people she hadn't spoken to in years, writing to lost loved ones, writing of hopes and dreams and fears and truths that she had never thought to stare.

She stopped when the ink pot ran dry, and stared at her work. That was… something.

Quickly, she sorted the letters into two piles: those to be sent, and those to be immediately burnt in the fireplace.

With that job done, Liesl collected Amie and her best trimmed bonnet and set out to see the sights of Brightside.

If she was out of the house, at least Emma could not ask awkward questions about whether Liesl had figured out which of Emma's closest friends might have snaffled a family jewel.

What could be so difficult about it? Liesl's friends Mneme and Juno were constantly solving something or other, with the occasional help of their dashing husbands. They made it look so easy.

She would write to them and ask their advice, but Mneme was on her honeymoon, and Juno expecting, and they probably had little interest in her minor family mystery.

"Lady Liesl! Wait up!"

No sooner had Liesl and Amie set foot on the path towards the town than there was a cry behind them. Liesl spun her parasol around to find Miss Indigo Larkin hurrying towards them. She looked far more the young lady today, less the paint-spattered urchin, in pale blue muslin and a matching parasol. Her wild golden curls were pinned up tidily in an arrangement similar to Liesl's hair. They could be mistaken for sisters.

Actress, Liesl reminded herself. Butter might not melt in

Indigo's mouth now, but this young lady had been far less friendly the first time they met. Still, she could meet sweet with sweet. "Miss Larkin," she said as if this was the greatest joy she could imagine. "Will you walk with us?"

"I'd love to," said Indigo, her cheeks rosy. "Emma — that is, the Countess thought you might like someone to show you the promenade, and the pier. Brightside has so many amusements."

So, Emma knew Liesl was fleeing the scene of the crime, and had sent her a suspect to interrogate. No wonder the lady had married so well: she was sharp as a pair of ribbon scissors.

Liesl smiled her friendliest smile and took Indigo's arm, the two of them walking ahead with Amie behind them. *Model, muse and dear companion* were the words Emma had used to describe this young lady. "How did you and my stepmother meet? I must know every detail."

"If you must know," said Indigo, with a laugh that was at least half-feigned. "She and Perdita fished me out of a pond."

"No!"

"Yes. Indeed. I was modelling for Gordon Falstaff — terrible man, brilliant artist. He wanted me to pose for a painting of Drowned Grisella, you know that play."

"Blue among the bulrushes," quoted Liesl, frowning. "Pity poor Grisella, doomed to the deep."

"That's the one! So I was lying in a pond while he painted me for oh, hours. I was so cold I couldn't speak, couldn't move. And he always flew into the most frightful temper when I interrupted him…"

Liesl's mouth fell open, and she saw Amie behind her, similarly startled. "So you just lay there?"

Indigo nodded, tears hovering on her eyelashes. "By

the time I realised I should say something, I could barely move my fingers. But the Countess and Perdita happened past — this was a public park — and they set on him, shouting blue murder as they pulled me out. Wrapped me in blankets and took me home. I never saw Gordon again." She pulled a face. "He won a prize for that painting. I think he left for the Continent to spend all the money — and to escape Emma bad-mouthing him in public, which had become her favourite game."

Their walk took them past the cliff-edge with its dazzling view of the ocean and the little township below. The buildings were quite extraordinary, arranged in rows, all pink bricks and sandstone, with yellow-tiled roofs that made the whole town look like the most elaborate sand-castle. Liesl could see the pier: a long extension of the town out to sea, featuring bright colours and lanterns. Little sailing boats and paddle boats fanned out in patterns. There were bathing machines, too: elaborate metallic spheres with articulated legs, or wings like owls.

"So you simply moved in?" Liesl asked. "What good friends they are."

"Perdita needed a model for her dryads," said Indigo. "It was easier to live here while she worked. And Emma — the Countess, well. She's so splendid, isn't she? There's always something to do around here. Some way to be useful."

Must be nice, Liesl thought. "And my father," she said aloud, remembering how defiantly Indigo had called him George, the night before. "You know him well."

"Oh yes," said Indigo. "He's a jolly good sort, your father. Always game for a laugh."

It was the most outlandish statement Liesl had ever heard in her life. She was not easily startled, but this had her beaten.

(The Earl had been caught laughing in that marble bust in the library, but surely that was a figment of Perdita's imagination, not sketched from life.)

"Indeed," she murmured, attempting to cover her confusion.

What would this girl know about the Earl of Sandwich, anyway? She couldn't even get out of a pond on her own.

~

By the time they reached the town of Brightside, Liesl had coaxed Indigo into telling further amusing tales of her life as a model and muse. Amie, fascinated, crept forward until the three of them were walking abreast. The maid had even got up the courage to ask a few questions of her own.

At this rate, Liesl would lose Amie to a life of oil paints and fishponds.

"Have you really never been to Brightside before?" Indigo asked in a careless tone as they passed a fine terraced street adorned with geranium pots, with children playing on nearly every door stoop.

"Not once," said Liesl. "Our family trips to Bath were on the other side of the island."

There were countless popular resorts on the fashionable side of Bath: Liesl's mother had favoured Audley, though Halford and Sheringham were much the same. Quaint little towns furnished with all manner of adult amusements from the pump rooms and magic shows to the lending libraries — and for the children, puppet shows on the pier, sweet rock, charmwork contests and donkey rides.

In between every town, a series of spa resorts and sulphur hamlets, so that no one could go more than a couple of miles without the opportunity to engage in healthful waters, fumes or treatments.

Liesl's older sisters had talked of the balls and assemblies. Anna and Retta both came Out in the grand Assembly Rooms at Audley. Gerda's was held in Town, though she often said wistfully that she would have felt less terrified if she had followed in the footsteps of their sisters.

By the time Liesl came out, their mother was gone and their father no longer wished to share his Bath amusements; he had Aphrodite Villa and Emma tucked away all to himself.

"We're smaller here, of course," said Indigo, speaking as if she was a native resident. "Not as many social engagements as you might find to the west. Not as much magic, either — for some reason the really popular exhibits never travel this far. But there's a splendid promenade overlooking the sea, a darling little funfair on the pier, and a new lending library coming this winter."

"You intend to still be here in winter?" said Liesl, surprised. She had thought her stepmother was hosting an overlong house party, not establishing a permanent household here at the seaside, away from her husband.

Indigo looked quite indignant. "Why, where else should we go, in Emma's hour of need?"

"I was not aware Emma's hour of need was anticipated to last so long," said Liesl, feeling brittle.

The promenade was indeed reasonably splendid: a very pretty avenue with quaint little shops, several temples and shrines (all dedicated to Apollo or Artemis only, none at all to Aphrodite or the rest of the pantheon, an odd sort of imbalance) and a long line of trees to shelter one from the whipping wind. It might be summer, full sun shining, but the easterly wind went direct to the bones through Liesl's white muslin.

The promenade gave way to the pier she had seen from above, jutting out into the water. It was larger than Liesl had expected, and covered in stalls and amusements. Not quite the massive funfairs of the fashionable side of the island, but jolly enough. There were games and trinkets for sale, and merry crowds wherever they looked.

Magic, too: no one seemed to be holding back from enchantments and illusions this close to the water like they did at Aphrodite Villa. Still less magic than you would find in most spa towns, though, and most of it was small; unambitious.

Amie and Indigo swarmed the coconut shy, with an unfiltered joy that made Liesl suddenly, fiercely long for the company of Clytie, her youngest sister.

Oh, Clytie would adore playing detective.

"You've been asking a lot of questions," said a male voice, very near.

Liesl jumped slightly, then regained her composure. "Mr Merryweather."

Merry the Poet King in his beard and peasant clothes. He leaned against a nearby nut stall, regarding her with a steady sort of suspicion. He might have been handsome, if his beard was tidy, but it looked rather as if a team of badgers had been attempting to built a nest in it. "Do you have any questions for me, Lady Liesl?" he asked.

She straightened her shoulders, refusing to be cowed. (How did he know she had been asking questions of Indigo? Had he followed them the whole way?) He had given her the opening: she ought to seize it. "Why do you live with my stepmother?"

"To save money," he replied, gaze locked on hers. "We make excuses, of course. We like each other's company, we're worried Emma is lonely now her beast of a husband has shown his true colours. But the truth is, staying here saves us coin, and none of us have much to spare. We're artists, you know. Constantly broke, even at our height of success."

Liesl arched an eyebrow at him. "And is there any particular reason that one of you might need money especially? This month, for instance. *As a matter of urgency*."

Mr Merryweather spread his hands wide. "So you want to know all our dirty laundry? I don't think we're intimate enough for that, Lady Liesl."

"Just tell me yours," she said, feeling bold. "Why might you feel especially desperate for money right now, Mr Merryweather?"

He gave her an odd sort of smile, half-buried beneath the beard. "No particular reasons except the obvious ones you would uncover if you asked around."

Liesl asked no further questions. That was her mother's old trick, if someone was being obstreperous. One waited them out.

She smiled at him, straightened her dress, and waited.

She didn't know many writers, but she was fairly sure that most of them preferred to fill silence where possible.

"I write better here than in Town," Mr Merryweather burst out after a few moments. "Don't ask me why. I've written reams since I've been here. Lines and lines. Wonderful stuff. If I return home it's back to me and the blank pages all over again. I have the greatest poem of my life still to write, and I can't afford to lose my flow if the Countess of Sandwich tosses us out on our ear."

"Why would she do such a thing, if she is such a generous friend?" They all seemed comfortable together, from what Liesl could see. But of course, a certain stolen jewel might change all that. Had one of their friends hoped to sabotage the Poet King?

Mr Merryweather's smile had disappeared now. "Even

the most generous of friends starts to reassess the parasites in her life," he said in an ominous tone of voice. "…Once there's a baby on the way."

Liesl took pride in not being easily startled, but that particular revelation shook her to the bone.

6

SHELL-SHOCKED WITH SEA SHELLS ON THE SEASHORE

FROM: *LADY LIESL BATTENBURG-SEVILLE OF SANDWICH, APHRODITE VILLA, BRIGHTSIDE, THE ISLE OF BATH*

TO: *THE DUCHESS OF STORM, STORM BOLT, THE ISLE OF TOWN, OR POSSIBLY STORM NORTH, THE ISLE OF STORM.*

*M*y dear Juno,

~~I am most discombobulated~~
~~You would not believe what is going through my~~
~~Of all the~~
~~I am ashamed of my~~
~~I wish I sailed through the world as effortlessly as you~~
~~seem to~~

Thank you for sharing your recent news about the expansion of your family. I wish you and Henry nothing but the best.

I am about to embark upon a splendid mystery involving jewel theft, family secrets and a horde of thoroughly scandalous side characters. I would share the author's name with you, but the tale is still being written…

Much to tell. I look forward to sharing tea with you soon.

Your friend,
Liesl

~

*L*iesl needed to speak with Emma as a matter of urgency, but she did not get the chance. When she returned to Aphrodite Villa with Amie and Indigo, she found the house completely empty of stepmothers or suspects.

"The ladies are bathing," Tavistock informed her, giving an unimpressed sniff in the direction of Amie, who was windblown and happily holding a coconut, thereby not behaving as a lady's maid should.

Torquay the butler, as usual, was nowhere in sight. Liesl was starting to wonder if Amie had made him up.

"Bathing," Liesl repeated. "In the *sea?*"

This was the Teacup Isles; every child could swim. Liesl's boarding school had been surrounded by rock pools, with sea-bathing a favourite pastime of the girls. But splashing and fun and throwing seaweed at each other was one of those things young ladies were supposed to put away when one came Out in Society, because suddenly it was all about frocks and hair and the appearance of perfection.

That must be one of the benefits of being married, she had always thought. You no longer had to worry about what people thought of you. Apparently it was also a benefit for those who were already considered scandalous.

"Oh, do let's!" cried Indigo. "It's as warm as anything at this time of day."

Liesl glanced at her maid. "I don't suppose…"

"No thank you, milady," Amie said hastily. "I'm happy with my coconut. You go on and enjoy yourself."

Enjoy yourself. Well, why not? And it would give her clever maid a chance to further their investigations. After all, no one was better at observations than those who worked Downstairs.

~

There was a private beach directly below Aphrodite Villa: that is, it was probably supposed to be private, but the family had done nothing to prevent locals from enjoying it. Quite a few onlookers, many with children, wandered around the sands, eyeing the party from the villa with open curiosity. Some, more tight-mouthed than others, steered their children away so that they might not be corrupted by the presence of disrep-utable outsiders. Others, mostly those without children to concern themselves about, merely gaped open-mouthed.

And no wonder.

Emma and Perdita were garbed in the most outlandish striped gowns, tight fitting at the sleeves and neck, with bunching knickerbockers below. Liesl had seen people wearing such garments at various seaside resorts over the years, but never anyone she *knew*.

Her only public bathing since she turned fifteen was in formal indoor bathing establishments, such the marble baths beneath Wistworia Palace. Here, Emma had hired a machine shaped like an enormous owl; a most outlandish contraption with spindly articulated legs and wings, designed to deposit ladies in deeper water without them being so undignified as to wade a little in the shallows.

One would not wish to be undignified.

It was oddly refreshing to taste magic again: everyday charms scattered here and there over the beach. Tiny spells for preventing sun-burn, for keeping lemonade chilled, for protecting one's towels or underthings from gritting up with sand. It felt familiar and warm in a way that the villa, where such charms were barely used (or barely worked) did not.

There were pastel-painted bathing huts all along the sands, and Liesl found herself hustled into one in order to change her respectable white muslin into a thick maroon garment that covered more of her limbs and yet felt entirely, absurdly scandalous.

The garment was paired with stockings which went to her knees, preventing her from shocking anyone with a flash of her bare feet.

At least her bathing suit had no stripes, which would be a shade too far.

Still, she felt rather ridiculous as she emerged blinking into the midday sunshine.

"See how respectable we are?" Perdita breathed into Liesl's ear as she helped her inside the large wooden shape of the bathing machine. It bulged in the middle, like a barrel about to burst. "Before you came, we confined ourselves moonlight swimming in nothing at all."

"If you're trying to make me blush," said Liesl steadily. "I'm afraid you'll be disappointed." She sat beside Emma on a narrow bench, the two of them opposite Perdita and Indigo.

"Well?" Emma asked in an murmur. "What have you discovered so far?"

"Your friends all need money," Liesl replied, just as quietly. "They all seem to adore you. Oh, and apparently you're *with child*."

Emma gasped. There was the blush Perdita had been after, staining the wrong cheek.

Liesl turned to Indigo politely, as if nothing had been spoken between her stepmother and herself. "So how exactly does this machine get us out into the water? It is too much to hope it's a litter with pretensions?"

Indigo giggled. "It has wings, doesn't it?" she said. "What a waste if it didn't fly."

Liesl had been rather afraid of that. She was glad she had not insisted Amie accompany her. Her poor maid had been through enough.

"Oh dear," drawled Perdita, not looking the slightest bit sorry. "Emma. Didn't you warn her?"

～

*T*he bathing machine did indeed fly. Liesl gained no benefit from the marvellous view the others squealed over, for she was too busy trying to stay upright, shaken this way and that by the ungainly lurching. Just because it was possible to build a magical bathing machine that looked like a giant metal owl did not mean it had the same grace and finesse of the bird it was shaped after.

Once they settled on the surface of the water, the bathing machine became a mere hut again, its wings spread wide to keep the contraption stable.

Emma went first, dropping into the water as if she could not get away from Liesl fast enough. There would be no covert chats between them any time soon. Indigo went next, eager to mimic Emma as always.

Perdita hesitated on the threshold, treating Liesl to her

warm smile and unblinking cat's eyes. "Would you be offended, Lady Liesl, if I asked to sketch you?"

"For one of your murals?" asked Liesl, thinking of the nymphs and dryads currently cavorting around the breakfast room.

Perdita shrugged. "A sculpture, perhaps. Who knows? You'd look well in marble, I think, if I could afford the stone."

"And are you so short of money?" Liesl dug.

Perdita frowned. "What an unladylike question. I'm quite offended."

"No offence was meant," said Liesl. "It has occurred to me that all of my stepmother's friends are reliant on her kindness for roof and board. And you're all settled here, as if for a terribly long time."

"Has it occurred to you all on your own?" purred Perdita. "No one has been talking out of turn?"

Liesl could name Mr Merryweather, but chose not to. "What would your financial situation be, if the Countess withdrew her support?"

"I would be devastated to lose her friendship," said Perdita, her voice as hard as Liesl's. "But I would still be a notorious genius with a steady work ethic, and no expensive habits. I am sure I could sell something."

"What would you miss, about Aphrodite Villa?"

"Apart from your charming presence?" Perdita said, all flirt gone from her voice. "I hadn't thought about it. It's just a house."

"Mr Merryweather said he writes better here than in Town."

"What an extraordinary thing for him to say. I suppose I have been producing more work than usual over the last few weeks. But that's only natural, without having to bother about meals and cleaning and so on. I do enjoy all the natural light. I wake up earlier. And…" An odd look crossed her face.

"And?" Liesl pressed.

"And I always wake up brimming with ideas," said Perdita slowly. She sniffed and tossed her head. "But that's the life of an artist, don't you know. So much inspiration we haven't the time to deal with it all."

"Why do you want to sketch me?" Liesl pressed.

"Your face when astonished," Perdita said, recovering some of her poise. She smirked a little. "It is quite a fascinating thing. Worth capturing."

"After today," Liesl muttered. "I don't think I should be surprised by anything ever again. Let alone astonished."

"The day is still young," said Perdita, stepping off the bathing machine so that she plunged into the icy brine below. Her hair ballooned around her in the water, wide and dark.

Liesl could not look away.

~

*B*athing was hardly the end of it. No sooner had the ladies immersed themselves decoratively in the salt water than Emma had them wading back to the sand where fresh clothes were waiting at the bathing huts. There was a local sandcastle contest to be judged (for those locals who did hustle away in alarm at the appearance of the Bohemian housemates) and after that, a brisk walk along the beach to collect seashells. The gentlemen of the household were allowed to join them for the picnic that followed. After the picnic, another walk. After the walk, tea back at the villa.

Considering the skeleton staff of Aphrodite Villa, the afternoon ran remarkably smoothly, from one event to another, never a time to catch your breath, and always a plate of cakes or cup of tea at your elbow should you want it.

It was as if the whole day was designed for Emma to avoid being alone with Liesl, and for Liesl to struggle even to take a moment with her own thoughts.

A *baby*. Did the Earl know? Was that why he was so furious about the diamond, about the possibility that Emma was preparing to leave him for good? Or was it merely a matter of bad timing?

Had Emma stolen the jewel after all, to set herself up for a husbandless pregnancy?

"Did you enjoy your day, Lady Liesl?" Basil Robucks inquired over a warm supper of ham and greens. He was dressed all in black again, though an entirely different suit. His cuffs were beaded; his coat tailored so tightly that he might be a fainting risk.

"Indeed," she said, reaching for her glass of lemon water. "I have seen so much of the local sights I fear I shall never need to visit again."

The lemon water left a tang of fizzing sulphur in the back of the throat. Liesl winced and swallowed it down. Better to drink from the local springs than to start sipping seawater, which was all the rage as a health tonic on the fashionable side of Bath, and never a pleasure to find at the supper table.

"Many of us are here for health or inspiration, not the tourist traps," said Basil, sipping his own beverage without issue. Either he and the others had grown accustomed to the strange flavours that came with 'taking the waters,' or Liesl's glass had been heavily doctored.

"And which are you here for?" Liesl asked. "Your health, or your work?"

It seemed odd for an art critic and famous fashion

leader to find himself so settled in the back of beyond. Surely his work drew him for Town and Court, not Brightside.

Basil raised his glass to Emma, toasting her health. "It is the only place I would wish to be," he said, eyes sliding back to their hostess. "Isn't she simply marvellous?"

Oh yes. The Countess's friends clearly all thought so. And yet, one of them had betrayed her.

Emma clapped her hands. "An announcement!" she declared. "I am preparing a gift for you all, my dear friends. Three nights from now, I shall perform the Classics!"

Everyone hooted and clapped as if this was a delightful treat.

Liesl returned to her dinner.

"You're in for something special, Lady Liesl," Basil assured her. "Emma puts on an unforgettable show."

Liesl felt weary of them all. These so-called Bohemians, these rebellious artists, all so desperate to skirt the levels of what was proper, and what was scandalous. Why should she observe the rules of society in their company by beating around the bush? "Are you in love with my stepmother, Mr Robucks?" she asked brutally.

Basil, beautiful jackdaw that he was, blinked several times. "Upon my word. Merry is right, Lady Liesl. You do ask the most *extraordinary* questions."

After that, he devoted all his supper conversation to Perdita Cholmondley, and pretended that Liesl herself did not exist.

7

DRAWING CONCLUSIONS

*T*hat night, as she let down Liesl's hair, Amie reported in what she knew of the movements of the villa's occupants. "Miss Larkin's been nowhere in a month, Bets the tweeny told me that she barely stirs away from the villa most days, and never without the Countess of Sandwich at her side."

"She did today," Liesl remarked. "She came bathing with us, and all the other seaside things. And she walked to Brightside with us before that."

Amie rolled her eyes at her. "And wasn't it all at the Countess' bidding? Them downstairs reckon Miss Larkin thinks her Ladyship walks on water."

Liesl nodded. "I can't work out if Indigo's in love with her, or somehow wants to murder her and take her place."

"Bit of both, I reckon," said the maid. "Now, that Mr Robucks, he has all manner of parcels going back and forth to the post office on the North Coast, where we arrived, miss. From his tailor in Town, but it sounds like he sends back clothes for mending and washing as often as he receives new outfits."

Liesl frowned. "Didn't you say he had a valet here?"

"Oh yes, but you've never seen such a lazy creature as Mr Evans. And Mr Robucks has said apparently that there's something about the waters here that's, uh, 'unkind to silk thread' so he won't have his things washed on the island. Have you ever heard anything so silly?"

"It certainly sounds like he could easily have smuggled a necklace to Town."

"That's what I thought! Also Evans the footman, he's got a bit of a loose tongue when he's been at the supper beer."

"Has he now," said Liesl.

"He said that Mr Robucks was due back to Town weeks ago. He's cancelled all these engagements and appointments. So many letters come, every day. Evans said he's in danger of losing his reputation as the most fashion-able man about Town, being away so long. There have been three art openings of very famous artists, where he was expected to turn up and say really quite rude things about the artwork, and since he didn't bother to attend, all the invitations are starting to dry up. By the time the next Season starts, he might be Yesterday's News."

"How dreadful," noted Liesl thoughtfully. Was Basil trying to sabotage his own public reputation? Why was he here? Did he really think Emma might leave her husband for him? (Had she already? There was no sign of an actual attachment between them, for all his lovelorn looks in her general direction.)

"And there's more," Amie went on. "Mr Merryweather, he has these massive sulks when he picks fights with the others at breakfast, then goes wandering about the coun-tryside, sometimes for days."

"Long enough to get himself to a portal and back again."

"Three times over, yes miss."

Liesl had to ask, though she felt oddly traitorous doing so. "And what about Miss Perdita Cholmondley?"

Amie consulted the notes she had made. "She only left Brightside once in the last few weeks, with the Countess and Tavistock, and they did go to the post office, but Tavistock swears they only collected a parcel — some watercolour pencils, I believe. The rest of the time, they visited a tea room and a hat shop, never out of each other's company."

"So," Liesl said. "It looks like one of the gentlemen, then."

"At least we've narrowed it down, miss." Amie looked delighted with herself.

Liesl patted her on the shoulder. "You've done brilliantly. I do appreciate it. And I'm rather glad it's not… one of the Countess's intimate female friends."

Glad it's not Perdita, she thought to herself. Indigo… well. Indigo Larkin was a whole other matter. Liesl would continue to be suspicious of her, even if she was now fairly certain the girl was not the one who had stolen the necklace from Emma.

Basil or Merry. Merry or Basil.

❦

The morning of Emma's performance dawned at Aphrodite Villa. Liesl had now been here several days. Several days of asking questions and making a nuisance of herself, while Emma avoided her and Bohemians made art in every room.

The artists were friendlier than they had been, though they also seemed to be making a game of answering her questions in ways that made Liesl suspect they were outright lying to her about literally everything. Unless it was true that Mr Merryweather once travelled to the Continent to write a series of sonnets about a slight famous elephant...

Their lives were to bizarre to her, how was she to tell truth from lies?

And every morning, Liesl lay awake for a few minutes, staring at the ceiling, and willing herself not to write letters.

Spending an hour or two (or three) in the morning, reading and writing correspondence, was one of those ladylike obligations that had been drilled into her since she was very young.

She had never especially enjoyed writing, or reading books which did not have pirates in them, but from the age of six she had been dragged into libraries and parlours and morning rooms by her Grandmamma to pass blotters and ink bottles to her, and to practice her own delicate, ladylike handwriting alongside her elder sisters.

Mamma had flat out refused to join them. "One day a week to catch up on the more interested exploits of old school chums and to refuse all unnecessary information, and one day a month to order seedling catalogues and peruse the broadsheets and that's all anyone can expect of me," she said, sailing past the Eggshell Library on her way to the garden, with a basket full of secateurs and her sturdy manure-waders on. "I have my limits."

"Humph," Grandmamma had said, once she was sure that Ana Margareta and her secateurs were out of the range of hearing. "And she calls herself a Countess."

Somehow it had never occurred to Liesl that she, like Mamma, could say no to such duties. Not with Grandmamma glaring at her through that terrifying monocle.

No wonder the current generation of young wives and

mothers had chosen to spend their dedicated 'correspondence hours' writing melodramatic novels at each other instead of arguing with their mothers-in-law.

"I don't need to write letters today," Liesl told herself today, as she slipped out of bed and called Amie to come help with her hair. "It's an unnecessary habit. Once I'm back in Town I shall be able to use portals again to pop in on the friends I actually like, and the rest of them can carry on writing to each other. I'm sure they'll hardly even notice my absence."

The letter-writing was starting to unsettle her. Far from her usual perfunctory notes, since she first came to the villa she had been writing bucketloads, hearthloads of letters. Most of them only fit for the fire, as they were full of so many of her real feelings, the outpourings of her soul, and no one needed to see that next to their boiled egg of a morning.

It felt so good to throw her feelings on the page but afterwards she felt quite sick about it, mostly because she had not intended to write them at all.

Something was…

It was as if…

Was this what inspiration felt like? She did not care for it at all.

FROM: *LADY LIESL BATTENBURG-SEVILLE OF SANDWICH, APHRODITE VILLA, BRIGHTSIDE, THE ISLE OF BATH*

TO: *THE DUKE OF STORM, STORM BOLT, THE ISLE OF TOWN, OR POSSIBLY STORM NORTH, THE ISLE OF STORM, BUT ACTUALLY IT DOESN'T MATTER WHERE YOU AND JUNO ARE, THIS ONE'S NOT GETTING POSTED.*

I should take actually the address off altogether, I'm asking for some kind of comedy of errors disaster situation where it ends up getting posted to the recipient despite my express wishes.

*D*ear ~~Henry,~~
Dear Nameless Man I Nearly Married,

It occurs to me, the more I am learning about myself, that while I would have made an excellent Duchess, I would in my heart have been desperately unhappy married to you. I might not have even understood why, for many years to come.

~~Therefore, thank you for choosing a more suitable wife.~~

I have an apology to make to you. I'm tired of writing, my fingers are sore and the pen-nib makes a most irritating noise as it scratches across the paper.

I can't stop myself. I have to keep writing my feelings, on papers I tear up and others I put into the post obediently, as I was trained to do.

This one is not going into the post.

Still, you are owed an apology. This one doesn't count, blotted and tired and forced though it is. Some time soon, I'll find a moment at one of your many parties and take you aside, say my piece. I expect you'll be kind about it.

We all treated you as a prize to be won. Schemed over you, simpered over you, performed various acts of small but significant magic upon you, in order to manipulate your choice.

That craving, that compulsion to be married, to capture the eligible Duke, to shape one's future around a partnership with a person one has not even met yet… this is the world we live in, women like me. I'm tired of it. Tired of myself. Tired of thinking that is all we can ever expect for ourselves.

My sisters made good marriages. My father made a good marriage, followed by a scandalous marriage, the latter to a woman I have more time for than any of my dull and respectable brothers-in-law.

I'm still looking for what I want. It's not you. It was never you. I might as well have married an oil painting of an eligible Duke with kind eyes and a good leg.

I have a lot of thinking to do.

Your friend,

Liesl

❧

*I*t had taken three days of squabbles, teasing, flirtation and banter, but Liesl had finally agreed (or had she?) to allow the infamous genius, sculptor and muralist Perdita Cholmondley to sketch her in the music room.

She was not sure why the Earl and Countess should have a music room in their home. Her father had always declared that orchestral instruments were a waste of floor space… but of course, the version of her father who married Emma was an entirely different Earl of Sandwich to the one Liesl knew.

Still, did anyone need two harps *and* a pianoforte? It seemed excessive, and quite a challenge for a small household staff to keep dusted.

Not that there was a speck of dust anywhere, on any of the instruments. Perhaps the imaginary butler played them in his spare time.

Liesl found it unnerving, to sit under close observation. She had not been examined so minutely since her first appearance at Belverdene, an exclusive club in Town reserved only for those ladies awarded a coveted voucher by one of its patrons.

She sat on the stool of the pianoforte, her back straight and her muslins pristine. Perdita the professional artist was far less flirtatious than Perdita the indolent house guest, and somehow that was even more terrifyingly attractive.

When those piercing cat's eyes of hers locked themselves upon a freckle on Liesl's elbow or the sideway curve of her ankle, it made Liesl shiver with pleasure. She knew from Perdita's slight frown that her thoughts were on artistic problem-solving, not salacious intent, and why did that make Liesl want to make her smile all over again?

Well, she was starting to suspect why of course she felt such a thing. This visit really had been full of surprises.

Without a witty exchange of conversation to entertain her, Liesl found her eyes drawn to the walls of the music room. Another Cholmondley fresco, this one so new she could still smell the paint. On one colourful green band around the top of the walls, the god Apollo frolicked with a host of shepherds and lyre players. On the blue band below, his sister Artemis hunted what looked like deer but on closer examination were also shepherds and lyre players. Her bow and hair were bright with freshly-applied gold leaf.

"I've sold a commission," Perdita said, half an hour into their session. "A nameday portrait of the Queen, in marble. I had it confirmed in writing two weeks ago. It's a gift from Lord and Lady Manticore, for her Majesty — she will sit for me this winter."

"That sounds marvellous," said Liesl, not sure what else to say. "Such an honour."

"Oh yes," said Perdita with an arch smile, not looking up from her sketch-book. "Paid in advance. Quite enough to see me through the season in Town, and the summer after. So you needn't ask me further questions about my financial situation."

It was days since Liesl had done such a thing. In truth, she had run out of questions to ask, and had merely spent the last day or so getting to know each of the artists in turn. "I don't believe I asked any questions of you recently," she said.

"No," mused Perdita. "That's true. But I haven't worked out yet why you're here. I caught Emma crying yesterday."

"Oh." Liesl bit her lip. "I'm sorry to hear that. I know things are difficult for her right now."

"Are they." Perdita swayed back and forth before her sketch book like she was about to fling it aside and pounce. "I don't suppose you can tell me anything?"

"I wouldn't break a confidence!"

"Of course not." Perdita frowned. "Is it your brother, your sisters, or your father?"

Liesl tilted her head slightly; a mistake. Perdita tsked at her, and Liesl moved it back hurriedly. "Whatever do you mean?"

"I know none of you have ever given Emma the time

of day since she married the Earl, but she always said you were the only one of the children who didn't look at her like she had something foul-smelling on her shoe. If you're here, investigating her lifestyle and her friends and who spends her money, then one of them has convinced you she's not to be trusted. So. Your slimy brother, your horrid sisters, or your enraging, infuriating, fair-weather father?"

Perdita spoke lightly, as if the conversation was of no more import than paint colours.

"You've got me quite wrong!" Liesl insisted.

"Oh don't prevaricate, my dear. You have a very pretty face, but it does nothing of interest when you play pretend."

She thinks I'm pretty.

"I'm not trying to spy on Emma, or to… make her look bad," Liesl sputtered. "I'm trying to save her."

Perdita's eyes flashed with fury; she was like an avenging goddess, her pencil still flying across the page even as she argued. "From her gold-digging friends?"

No, not exactly. But of course that was what Perdita must think.

Liesl stood up. "If necessary, yes. You all seem to think you have her best interests at heart, but none of you are making her any happier, are you?"

She had spent what felt like a lifetime of politely exiting rooms. This was a solid 'storming out,' and she felt on the whole that she pulled it off most satisfactorily.

She heard a sound after the door slammed, which might well have been several pencils being snapped to pieces.

*A*nd of course, she felt wretched afterwards, hollowed out inside like she had lost something she had not even realised she wished for.

Her fingers twitched as if longing to pour out her heartsick whining on parchment paper, but she squeezed them tightly to her side and refused to bend. It wasn't even morning. Letters could wait.

❧

"*M*iss," said Amie later, as she dressed Liesl's hair for dinner. "Miss Tavistock says that me and Evans can serve in the parlour tonight, and that means we'll see her Ladyship's performance. Is that all right?"

"If you want to," said Liesl. "It's really not the done thing for them to ask you, Amie. You're an upstairs maid."

"Oh, I do want to! Mrs Pennance says it's a crime her Ladyship isn't still on the stage. They'll pay me, too… if you really don't mind."

"As you like." Liesl noted Amie's shining eyes. "You enjoy the theatre?" Amie had only been with her for a few months, since her last maid Hattie ran off to get married. Still, that meant Liesl had brought Amie through Town several times and never thought to ask what kind of entertainments she preferred. Anna and Retta and Gerda had boycotted theatres for years, ever since Emma fell into their lives — as if their own husbands might also fall prey to a stray juggler or ballerina. Apart from one trip to the opera last winter, at the Duchess of Storm's invitation, Liesl hadn't bothered with the theatres much herself, not wanting to give her sisters something else to criticise.

"I like the singing ones best," said Amie. "The funny

singing ones with kissing, not the solemn singing ones. Though I do like the very tragic ones with at least one pretty death and lots of daggers."

"Can't beat lots of daggers," Liesl murmured. She had a sudden thought. "Amie, so many of my friends from school are, uh, very attached to the trend for gothic mysteries. Murders and ghosts and secret passages, that sort of thing. Are they popular in plays too?"

"Oh, yes," said Amie, clearly delighted to talk about her favourite topic. "Sometimes it's the ladies who solve the mysteries, those are great fun! There's this one, where she was wearing a dress and a hat all in tweed and she kept saying 'the game's afoot!' and then coming up with solutions while waving her knitting around, I liked that very much."

"How do they end? I never quite get to the last chapters of my school-friends' novels, there are so many of them constantly arriving in the post that I drop one when the next comes along. How does the — mystery solving lady usually come to a conclusion?"

"In a drawing room," Amie said immediately. "They're ever so smart. The lady detective gathers the suspects in a room — a *drawing room* — and announces she knows whodunnit, and then she tells everyone's secrets out loud and the murderer tries to run away. It's very exciting."

"In a drawing room," Liesl said thoughtfully. "All the better to draw conclusions, I suppose. Well, I'll keep that in mind. Thank you, Amie."

"Happy to help, miss," said her maid, terribly cheerfully. "I am excited for the show tonight. Do you know what kind of show it is?"

"Not at all," said Liesl. "Hopefully not one of the tragic ones with lots of daggers."

8

AMBUSCADE

*a*fter supper, the suspects did indeed gather in a room, though Liesl could not say for sure that it was a drawing room. She had lost track of which rooms on the ground floor of Aphrodite Villa were parlours, receiving rooms, drawing or indeed withdrawing rooms. There were at least six of each, in different colour palettes, and the house was such a labyrinth that she was never entirely sure which room lay beyond which door.

In any case, no one was here to listen to theories about who had or had not stolen a valuable family diamond. They had gathered in the (alleged) drawing room for the same reason they had gathered in Aphrodite Villa in the first place: for Emma, the Countess of Sandwich.

Liesl had not known quite what to expect of Emma's showpiece: The Classics. A song or two, perhaps. Dancing? Something inappropriate, probably — or at least something that Grandmamma would have considered inappropriate, which included anything more daring than sitting very still while fully clothed.

Were there to be spangles? Ankle-revealing petticoat flutters? Jewels in unexpected places?

Nothing so outlandish, as it happened. When Emma entered the room she was dressed in a long white dress, covered in a light blue shawl. Very similar to what she had worn when Liesl first arrived at the villa, except that nothing was splashed in paint.

"Behold!" cried Mr Meredith Merryweather, his hands cupped around his mouth to create a vibrating intonation. "Her Fanciest Ladyship, Emma Lamb-Battenburg-Seville, Countess of Sandwich and Queen of our Hearts, performing her Classics!"

Their friends applauded wildly, but went respectfully silent once Emma stood before them. The guests sat in straight-backed chairs as the official audience, except for Amie and Evans the valet, who hovered at the back with a grinning Mrs Pennance, and Basil Robucks, who sat at a nearby piano with a herbal cigar clenched between his teeth.

Bert the stable lad was there too, Liesl realised, tucked into a corner behind the piano in the hopes no one would notice him. Bets the tweeny, in her cleanest apron, crouched beside him, eyes wide like saucers. So the entire household had turned out for the Countess' party piece except for the invisible butler and the maid of all work.

Basil began to play a slow, lilting melody.

Emma did not speak. She commanded their attention with her silence. She breathed slowly, in and out.

And then…

She transformed.

As the music rose and fell, the blue shawl became butterfly wings, a queen's mantle, the sail of a swan-shaped boat. It folded up to be a crown and a magister's hat and a harp between her fingers.

Emma changed too. Her face lengthened and short-ened, became ugly and beautiful, old and young. She pantomimed a host of characters from classical plays and ancient myth, from famous novels and plays and songs, each with a recognisable look and prop in her hands.

The audience broke their silence, calling out guesses as rapidly as she shifted from one character to another.

Was it magic, or not? At first Liesl was convinced that Emma was using some kind of enchantment, but magic didn't work that well in this house… and no, it was just cleverness. Acting. Posing. Expert performance and and folded fabric.

Basil's piano playing sped up, and Emma matched his speed. She was shifting characters every thirty seconds, then ten.

Her friends laughed and gasped and heckled her, utterly delighted. Captivated.

Liesl was captivated too. Such humour and cleverness and… a thought struck her.

She looked around, at the pride that shone from the faces of Basil and Merry and Perdita and Indigo. Emma's closest friends. In that instant, she knew that none of them would ever have betrayed her.

The faces of the staff were open and honest too, everyone from Mrs Pennance the cook to the stable lad behind the piano. Everyone thought the Countess was marvellous.

No, the mystery of the Prima-donna Diamond was to be solved elsewhere. And now, finally, Liesl had an idea where to start looking.

～

*D*uring the supper break, as Amie and Evans brought around trays of cheese and olives and other savouries, Liesl slipped away.

"Marvellous!" she heard Mr Merryweather exclaim as she made her discreet exit. "I thought marriage and conventionality would dim your star, my dear Lamb, but you're as magnificent now as you were the first time I saw you treading the boards at the Starlight Theatre."

"Glad not to disappoint," Emma said dryly. "Pass me an olive will you, Perdita my duck? I have to throw it at a poet."

"I do think the show's improved since I last saw it in Town," said Basil thoughtfully.

"Must be the sea air," said Indigo, without a touch of irony. "Makes everything taste better!"

∽

*L*iesl made her way through the green baize door and down a long white staircase towards the kitchens and servants quarters, beneath the ground floor. Because the villa was cut into the side of the hill on an angle, part of this floor had natural daylight, making it a vast improvement on most basement kitchens.

Still, the design was familiar enough. Liesl was searching for the room that would normally belong the housekeeper. Except, of course, Aphrodite Villa had no housekeeper. It had Tavistock, the maid of all work.

She found herself in an unexpected second scullery and turned back, only to find herself face to face a most determined Perdita Cholmondley. She was wearing a most fetching violet gown tonight, with very daring sleeves which Liesl had been trying not to notice.

"What are you doing here?" Liesl demanded in a startled whisper.

"What are you?" replied the artist, at a normal volume. "I hope you realise your behaviour is verging on skulking at this point."

"I'm not skulking," Liesl hissed, gesturing for Perdita to also lower her voice. "I'm investigating."

Perdita's eyes flashed. "This again. Your family really are the most outrageous—"

"Not Emma," Liesl said impatiently. "Someone is out to sabotage her marriage. There's this whole diamond business… anyway, I know now that you were right. None of her friends would try to hurt her. I should have realised earlier, and I'm sorry."

Perdita raised both eyebrows expertly. "So who do we expect? Are we about to ambush some scullery maid in her lair?"

"There are no scullery maids in this house," Liesl said impatiently. "Honestly, artists. You think the nobility are out of touch. Haven't you noticed that there are meals served every few hours, but barely a handful of servants, and no cleaning charms?"

"You wouldn't be able to use cleaning charms in this house," Perdita said dismissively. "Spells barely work."

"Exactly," said Liesl. "And yet, the dishes are clean." She waved a hand at the scullery which was indeed full of bright, gleaming white dishes and silverware. Not a servant in sight. "I've narrowed it down to Torquay and Tavistock. I've never even seen him, and she's the only one who doesn't stare at Emma like she's made of cake and twice as nice."

"You do come out with odd expressions," said Perdita. "But I'll grant you the butler is odd. I caught him out on the lawn once, chasing rabbits with a javelin."

"I thought I'd try Tavistock first," said Liesl. "But I'll keep in mind that that butler is… armed and dangerous. If I ever see him."

"Come on, then," said Perdita, swishing along the corridor.

"You're coming with me?"

"Naturally. You can't do this alone. I spend half my time lugging granite and marble and paintbrushes around — if she makes a break for it, you'll be glad to have a partner with powerful upper arm strength."

"Partner," said Liesl, doing her best not to blush. She had more important things to think about. Such as, how to ambush a maid of all work who seemed to be able to perform miracles.

⁓

*P*erdita, at least, knew the way to the housekeeper's parlour, set further back into the servant's quarters. The two of them approached the door with caution.

From inside, they could hear the tinkling of a piano, played with precision. The notes rose and fell in complex layers as if played by half a dozen virtuosos on several pianos.

"Is she having a party?" Perdita whispered.

Liesl knocked, and the music broke off.

Tavistock, a woman of exactly middle age, met Liesl at the door with a face so perfectly impassive, it belonged in a museum. She wore a pale dove grey dress covered in an enormous white apron, and a matching white cap. Neat as a pin.

"Lady Liesl," she said politely, with a face that

expressed no pleasure or annoyance. "Miss Cholmondley. May I help you?"

"We'll show ourselves in," said Liesl, barging into the room with Perdita on her heels. It was the rudest she had ever been to a member of staff in her life; her mamma had taught her to respect those who worked for you. Mind you, her mamma had also been one for barging everywhere if she had to go anywhere. "It's a big house, with many guests and barely another servant to hand," Liesl went on accusingly. "So much scrubbing and dusting and sweeping to be done, with no army of chamber and parlour maids to help you, and not a sniff of a cleaning charm in the air. You actually have time to practice piano?"

Tavistock smiled. It was not the smile of one who was concerned about her station in life. "There's not much to be done in a place like this. It practically runs itself."

"That's not how houses work," Liesl said impatiently.

"And you would know, of course. Milady."

"I know what cleaning charms smell like," Liesl replied haughtily. "And I know how many people it takes to keep a house this size running with or without them. Do you think girls of families like mine are taught nothing beyond fan-fluttering and simpering at eligible men? Managing a house is *what I was trained to do*."

Tavistock's eyes narrowed." And what do you know about this house, with all your expertise?"

"Anyone can tell something is wrong here," broke in Perdita. "Something about this house. I can't stop painting frescoes, but I can't make any of my paint spells work properly for love nor money. And I… I'm sure I'm supposed to be somewhere." She frowned. "Appointments in Town. The Queen's portrait… I'm sure I was supposed to be doing something about that."

Tavistock turned on her, eyes wide. "You're doing great work right here, miss. Aren't you?"

Perdita faltered. "I am doing great work, it's true. How kind of you to notice."

"You don't want to be anywhere else, do you? Not with so much fresh air and inspiration right here on your doorstep." The maid's voice was heavy, forceful. Liesl couldn't help agreeing with her. Of course Perdita should stay.

Perdita's eyelids drooped as if drugged. "So much inspiration," she murmured, then appeared to snap out of it. "Really, Liesl. Why would we want to go anywhere else? I've never been so inspired. I think I'll paint three frescoes tomorrow."

It made so much sense, and yet… and yet, Liesl had written so many letters she could paper a room with them. "Stop it," she snapped. "Stop whatever you're doing to her."

"I'm not doing anything, miss," said Tavistock.

"You are. And if it's not magic… it's something else."

When is magic not magic? When it…

Somewhere, a bell jangled. Tavistock twitched towards the door.

Liesl stood in her way. "No."

"I must get the door, milady."

"The butler greets guests, then the footman," Liesl said sharply. "Let them do it. Or, let one of them hire an appropriate number of staff to cover the available tasks. I'm not finished talking to you."

Tavistock's face went distant for a moment. "I have to go, milady. That's himself at the door. He's finally come back to us."

Liesl stared at her. "My father? How on earth would you know that?"

"Because IT'S MY HOUSE." Tavistock raised herself taller. She wasn't plain and middle aged at all, but quite beautiful. Young and beautiful and… familiar. Where had Liesl seen that face before? Tavistock looked like one of Perdita's marble busts, only with less of a sense of humour. "You are the intruder here," she thundered at Liesl. "I have to greet the master."

"No," Liesl said again, refusing to be tidied away. "Tell me about this house. Why was my father so desperate to have it built exactly here? How is it that Emma's friends are so inspired, so wildly attached to this place that they can't bring themselves to leave?"

Why can't I stop writing letters to people that pour out the truth after spending so many years keeping my thoughts to myself?

"And what have you done to Perdita?" she growled.

"Nonsense, Liesl, no one's done anything to me," said Perdita. "I could run laps of the house and build a mosaic at the same time. Actually, I think I could add some bas relief work to the downstairs lavatory, what do you think?"

The bell jangled again.

The maid threw her hands up in the air, like a magister casting enchantments.

Liesl staggered slightly, overcome by images that filled her head.

She was an opera singer on stage, holding a high note while adoring audiences threw orange blossoms at her feet. All her wishes come true.

She was a talented author, scribbling novels that her friends all gushed over, while bookshops sold them in lavish hardcover editions edged with gold. All her desires, met.

She was a sculptor, carving beauty out of cold marble, as the Queen herself arched her pretty chin to be copied. All her longed-for hopes, fulfilled.

81

She was a detective, earning the admiration of her family as she confidently declared "The murderer is…"

Liesl blinked, staring at Tavistock. "I don't want any of those things," she said. "And honestly, if you had all those to offer, why did you stick me with letter-writing for four days?"

The other women hissed at her, pulling an ugly expression with her beautiful, marble statue face. "Everyone wishes for something, sooner or later. What is your desire?"

Those were big questions, and Liesl was going to need some time to work them over in her head. "I don't know yet," she admitted." I've never been allowed to wish things for myself. That was supposed to come later."

After she secured the ideal husband, the successful estate, the approval of her father, the acceptance and unconditional love of her dead mamma and grandmamma… After she achieved perfection, as defined by the Battenburg-Seville family going back seven generations.

Even though literally no one was left in the family who cared if she did.

"Liesl, look out!" Perdita cried suddenly.

There was a blur of white as the statuesque maid of all work shoved past her and ran away, surprisingly fast.

Heart beating out of her chest, Liesl gave chase.

❧

*W*hen Liesl and Perdita made it back to the drawing/parlour/room, they were greeted by a frozen tableau. The Earl of Sandwich, still in his coat and hat, stood awkwardly on the threshold, pushing his way past a starchy-looking man in top hat and tails. The elusive butler Mr Torquay, perhaps?

Liesl blinked in astonishment as the butler turned to

her and winked. He was alive and moving. But the rest of them — every other person in the house — was stiff and cold. Unmoving.

The Earl's son (and Liesl's brother) Gustav, Viscount Ganymede, stood at his father's heels, face captured in an expression of fury.

What was wrong with them all? Had time been frozen, or had someone turned them into statues? To Liesl's great frustration, she still couldn't feel any traces of magic at all.

Bustled in behind the Earl and Gustav were the Earl's three eldest (and married) daughters, Lady Annabetha Battenburg-Seville Chisholm, Lady Margaretta Battenburg-Seville Sotheby, and Lady Gerdrut Battenburg-Seville Melusine. All three of them were dressed in fine gowns and new bonnets as if they expected to be at a royal picnic, or a public promenade. These were not gowns one chose to wear when visiting family, unless one meant to make a very specific impression.

An intense expression of disapproval was frozen on each of their faces, directed at... oh yes. The rest of the Bohemians had reassembled for the show. Basil was seated at the piano, leaving Indigo and Merry as an audience of two on the gilded chairs.

Emma, the Countess of Sandwich, stood on her makeshift stage, interrupted in the moment of an impersonation of Aphrodite, goddess of love. In her white gown, blue shawl and house slippers, she somehow managed to look as if she had recently stepped out of seafoam. Her expression was one of astonishment and sadness as she caught sight of her husband and his children, performing their surprise attack.

Emma's friends all tensed in their chairs, defiance captured on their faces. Indigo blazed with such indignation, she looked as if she was about to seize the nearest picture frame and batter the Earl around the head with it. Merry looked merely curious. At the very back of the room, Amie and Evans were caught in the moment of flattening themselves to the wallpaper, not wanting to be noticed by the horde of invading aristocrats. Bets and Bert had a better hiding place behind the piano. Mrs Pennance stared openly, clearly enjoying the show.

"You started without me," Tavistock complained to Torquay.

He rolled his eyes. "So impatient, sister. There's plenty of food to go around. Just look at them all."

"Spoilt for choice," she agreed.

"What have you done?" Liesl demanded of them both.

The two turned to stare at her. Brother and sister? Torquay, like Tavistock had an otherworldly beauty about his face. Pale like marble. Symmetrical, like a less than original artwork. The little moustache looked like it had been drawn on.

"They are quite safe," said the maid. "Caught in a moment between moments."

"Never mind that," Liesl said dismissively, waving away whatever incredible sorcery had turned a roomful of people into statues. "I want to know what you two did to my father."

"I don't follow."

"Do you not?" Liesl stood up very straight, facing down the maid who was not a maid. "Six years ago, my mother died. And the Earl, my father, he *changed*. Ran wild with theatricals and Bohemians. Fell in love. Eloped. My siblings all blamed Emma, but it started happening before that, didn't it? She's the symptom, not the disease."

"Charming stepdaughter you are," muttered Perdita at her elbow.

"Don't distract me by trying to make me feel guilty,"

sighed Liesl. "I'll do that later for myself." She turned back to Torquay and Tavistock. "Look at you both. You have some kind of power, enough to transformed him… oh."

When is magic not magic? When it performs miracles.

Liesl's eyes were drawn back to Emma, caught in her performance as Aphrodite. "Oh no."

"Look at you," said Tavistock smugly. "You solved the mystery."

"Wait," said Perdita. "That's not fair. Solve it out loud, for the rest of us."

"You didn't transform him," Liesl said slowly. "But you did *something*."

"We granted his wishes. His every desire. The beautiful house. The untouchable actress. Generations of debts paid. Arthritis pain vanished, overnight. A thinning hairline, verdant once more."

"We were kinder than he deserved," said Torquay. "Trespasser that he was."

"We haven't even made him pay the price… yet," said Tavistock. The two of them shared an inhuman giggle together.

Not the fey folk, not witches. Not magisters. No, it was worse than that. No wonder the house felt like a temple.

"You know the stories," Liesl said to Perdita. "The old myths. You've painted half of them. You know what they are."

"Oh, *gods*," said Perdita sucking in a breath as she realised.

Indeed.

Gods, walking the earth.

One knew such things happened in the olden days, of course, but no one had reported a sighting from the True Pantheon since Grandmamma was a girl, and most of those tales were hogwash anyway.

The inhabitants of the Teacup Isles preferred their gods to remain in their place: as the subjects of temple statues, naughty frescoes and overly-flowery poetry. No one was in any hurry to invite them around to tea.

(Or, heavens above, *to serve the tea.*)

Liesl was no longer merely surprised or startled or even astonished; she was outraged. Who did they think these two were, strutting among humans and playacting at maids and butlers? What was their game?

"Who are you?" Perdita asked Tavistock, the maid of all work. "This villa might be named after Aphrodite, but we haven't all spent the summer swooning at each other, so I don't think you're the goddess of love."

"No," the creature said with a tight smile. "Not love."

9

LIESL MAKES SEVERAL STARTLING ANNOUNCEMENTS; EMMA BRINGS THE HOUSE DOWN

"*I* suppose you're all wondering why I gathered you here," said Lady Liesl Battenburg-Seville of Sandwich, standing before a room full of family, friends, servants and suspects.

If it wasn't a drawing room before, it was now.

Tavistock had lifted whatever non-magic had frozen everyone in place; naturally, this caused something of a commotion.

"Where did you come from?" demanded Basil Robucks. "You weren't there a minute ago." He whirled around on the piano stool, staring at the window. "The moon's risen. What the hellfire is going on?"

"That's what I'd like to know," boomed the Earl of Sandwich. Liesl's father was a large man, with a commanding presence. Accustomed to being listened to, whenever he opened his mouth.

It had never quite occurred to Liesl before how very tiresome it was, that expectation. Perhaps because she was usually hoping he would notice her presence; today, she had other things on her mind.

"Emma, are you all right?" asked Perdita, ignoring the Earl.

Emma did indeed look paler than usual. She stepped back, stumbling a little. Perdita seized hold of her, guiding her to the couch. She wrapped her blue shawl tightly around herself and stared up at her husband.

"I need you all to listen very carefully," said Liesl, attempting to wrest back control of the room.

"Not now, daughter," the Earl said dismissively.

Liesl took a deep breath, summoning all the icy disdain of her grandmamma and all the brusque confidence of her mother. Ana Margareta had never crumbled before the Earl of Sandwich. She had nerves of steel and a backbone like a tree trunk. Liesl must have inherited some of that, surely. "Yes, now," she said, remaining calm but confident. "All of you. Gustav, Anna, Retta, Gerda. Father. Take a seat. I am going to speak, and you are all going to listen to what I have to say."

~

*M*y dear Clytie,

What a reunion you missed out on! All of our siblings, our father and stepmother, all gathered in the one place we have never been invited before: the legendary secret getaway. Aphrodite Villa. Honeymoon home, holiday house, love nest. Temple to… well, you'd be surprised.

There's a story to this house, and it's not easy to condense. But you deserve to know the truth.

It began when our father was widowed, and it ended… well. It hasn't ended yet.

If you happen to have a volume or two of mythological

poetry tucked away in your dresser, I suggest you dust it
off. It may prove rather useful…

~

*E*veryone shuffled themselves into a seating
arrangement: Evans and Amie brought some
more chairs for the ladies and gentlemen and then withdrew quickly, watching the whole scene with some alarm.

Tavistock and Torquay did not lift a hand to help, nor
did they sit among the gentry and the Bohemians. No
longer pretending to be servants, they lounged prettily on a
spare settee beneath the window, and smirked at each
other.

Despite their generally cryptic manner, they had
explained enough to Liesl that she now had a fair idea
what was going on, but they showed no sign of wishing to
help her communicate with the rest of them.

Perdita sat herself firmly down with Emma, leaving
Liesl in the spotlight.

Liesl had never drawn so much attention from so many
of her family members all at the same time. She almost
wished she had chosen a prettier dress. At least muslin
went with everything.

Perdita gave her an encouraging smile and a slow wink,
which warmed her. There was that, at least.

"After our mother died," Liesl began. "The Earl came
here, to Brightside. A town he had visited as a child. He
remembered it as a place where you could find happiness,
and toffee apples on the pier. He walked up here, on the
cliff, thinking about what he wanted from life, now he was
a widower."

"Now he was free," corrected Tavistock from where she

stood at the far wall. Her mouth twisted into a smile that was not exactly cruel, but certainly far from kind.

"No," Liesl said firmly. "You do not speak. You have had your turn. However this started, you are still bound to serve this household, and that means you will speak when you are spoken to."

Tavistock smirked at her, and mimed locking her mouth, throwing away the key.

The sisters looked horrified.

"Liesl," hissed Anna. "You can't talk to servants like that. Isadora Medley was snippy to her chambermaid last year and now she can't staff her house at *all*."

"Don't fret," said Liesl. "Tavistock isn't actually a servant. She's a deity bound into the human body of a maid, and there's a definite possibility that she'll have killed us all by the time I've stopped talking. So if you don't mind, I'll continue."

She did not look directly at her father, who was sitting stiffly with Gustav and Perdita sandwiched between himself and his wife. She could feel his presence, though, grumpy and disapproving. That at least was familiar.

"When he left Brightside," Liesl continued. "The Earl was a man inspired by art and life. He went to Town, and stayed there. Attending theatres and galleries and intellectual salons. He had fun, for perhaps the first time in his life. He fell in love, and managed somehow to convince a young, successful actress to leave the stage and marry him."

"Avoiding all family responsibilities," Retta said snippily.

"That part's nothing new," muttered Gerda.

The Earl's neck turned red, but he said nothing.

"And we all thought, didn't we," Liesl continued.

"What on earth has got into him? As it turned out, there was an answer: the gods."

"What rot," snorted Gustav.

"No," said Basil, waving a hand. "That makes sense. Is that why I can't leave this dratted house? I've cancelled six appointments with my tailor! And my reputation as an art critic is in the ditch."

"The cliff wasn't empty, you see," Liesl continued. "It held a marble temple, surrounded by laurel trees. And in that temple, a fountain. The first time the Earl visited this place as a widower, he discovered that the fountain granted wishes."

Emma pressed her hands to her mouth. "I'm going to be sick," she said distantly.

The Earl's neck was even more red than before. "You should stop talking now, daughter," he warned.

"Oh, am I going too far?" Liesl had not realised quite how angry she was at him until she started talking. Now, there was no holding back. She might never hold back again. "You wished upon a *fountain* in a *temple*, father. Not just one wish, either. You got greedy. You might have started out by wiping out a few debts, preserving the Abbey's roof from falling in — I wondered how it suddenly stopped leaking, that winter. But you kept going. You filled your coffers with wealth. You changed your hair, of all things. You —" Liesl hesitated for a moment, not wanting to make things harder on Emma.

But Tavistock telling her 'he wished to possess an actress who had never given him the time of day before' was not something she could ever unhear.

Did Emma know? Was that why she felt so much herself, living apart from her husband? Or was it being here that made her realise there was something wrong with her life? Here, at Aphrodite Villa.

Liesl went on: "You took their temple as your holiday home, transforming it to your own design. Named it after a different god, to add insult to injury. But you know how metamorphosis works. It doesn't matter if you change a shape. The original is always there, under the surface. Waiting to fight back. A temple doesn't stop being a temple because you added a few floors of guest rooms and added a pianoforte."

"You are hysterical," her father declared. "You can't prove any of this."

"I don't need to prove it," Liesl said, feeling rather exhausted. "I heard the story directly from the gods who granted your wishes. Your maid and your butler. Did you never notice that the floor remained clean though no one ever swept it? Or did you simply assume it worked that way because you've never had to think about such things before?"

Her brother Gustav, she knew, had not been forced through hours and hours of tutelage in household management as she and her sisters had done; no matter how many servants you hired, the mistress of the house was expected to understand the minutiae of every task in order to manage the whole business.

"Which gods?" interrupted Merry. He peered thoughtfully at Amie, who promptly hid behind Mrs Pennance. He then gave a good long squint to Mrs Pennance herself, before moving on. As his eye fell on the reclining Tavistock and Torquay, the butler waggled fingers at him in a sarcastic wave. Merry nodded, and scribbled something urgent in his ever-present notebook.

"Are you taking notes?" Indigo accused. "Now?"

"Naturally. This is going to make an excellent ballad."

"It's a work of art, that's for sure." said Perdita, giving Liesl an exasperated look. "So what do you think, Liesl?

Are we dealing with a certain god of music, art and inspiration?"

"Apollo was my first guess too," Liesl agreed. "You're not far off. They're his children, apparently. I don't know the story behind it…"

"Oh," said Torquay, rising to his feet and doffing his top hat. A long rope of black hair fell down behind him, decorated with leaves. "Did you want to hear our story?"

"They always leave us out of the ballads and frescoes," agreed Tavistock. She peered at Merry's notebook. "My name is spelled without an e at the end," she advised him.

"I was in the middle of something," said Liesl crossly.

"I want to hear it," said Emma.

Perdita squeezed her arm in silent sympathy.

Torquay circled the room, still in the polite and precise movements of an experienced butler, but there was a wildness to him now, visible along with the stillness. "You know how the gods are with mortals," he said in a sharp voice. "You've read the stories, painted the stories. One day, Apollo chased a woman who did not want him, and Daphne turned herself into a tree to escape."

Tavistock stood, walking to join her brother. "Apollo's sister Artemis, goddess of the hunt, made a habit of avenging the victims of men. She thought her brother deserved a little of his own medicine. So the nymph ran free, and the god was transformed in her place. A much better story, don't you think?"

"Laurel trees," said Emma with a gasp. "The house is surrounded with them… are you saying one of them is the god Apollo?"

"All twelve of them," said Tavistock. "Gods take up a lot of space."

"We were left behind," Torquay added. "The saplings. Abandoned by father and mother alike. Artemis left us here to guard the temple, watching over our father until she chooses to forgive him."

"It's been three hundred years," Tavistock said. "The trees grew. Our father rested. We became bored. So we allowed the occasional mortal to visit. Granted a few wishes. It passed the time."

"Preposterous," barked the Earl of Sandwich.

The divine siblings turned glowing eyes on him.

"No one ever wished more than three times," said Torquay. "No one used us as greedily you did. No one was as thankless, or graceless. We gave you everything. But you only saw us as servants, not gods. You never even said thank you."

"You cursed us," said Tavistock, her own voice ringing with disgust. "Placed a domestic loyalty curse upon us, as if we were *mortals*. To keep us loyal to your household. Such a short memory."

"This is our house," Torquay concluded, with a polite, withering smile worthy of several generations of butlers. "And the rent is due."

"Oh," said Gerda, quite dismayed. "*Father*. You can't go around cursing servants. People will talk."

"I think I preferred it when you were throwing away money on diamonds and actresses," agreed Anna

"I am right here in this room," snapped Emma.

"I knew it," Mrs Pennance the cook declared. "I knew that Tavistock woman had never swept a room a day in her life! And to think she took the housekeeper's room for herself."

Gustav, who had been silent up until now, stood up stiffly. "Is that what this has all been about? This is the excuse for Father's ridiculous indulgences, his mistress, all that money he's been spending of our inheritances like water..."

"It's not an inheritance until I'm dead," growled their father.

"Mistress?" said Emma, arching her neck to glare at her step-son. "You little toad. I am the Countess of Sandwich."

"Sit down, Gustav," Liesl advised him. "Sit down everyone. We're not finished here."

"We don't have time for you to suddenly grow a back-bone," Anna added snottily, tugging on their brother's sleeve. "I want to hear the rest. What exactly is the price of Father's folly?"

"That part, I don't know," Liesl confessed. She glanced at the perpetrators.

"He knows," mocked Tavistock.

"He's always known," agreed Torquay. "We were very clear."

"George," said Emma, as if bracing herself for hurt. "You must tell us. This affects the whole family. What have you done? What have you *promised?*"

"I never thought... I didn't take them seriously," the Earl blustered. "Contracts, payments. All that mundane business. There's always a loophole. My mother didn't pay a butcher's bill for twenty five years, and the farmers kept delivering the best beef to the house. Our sort of people don't..."

"Don't face consequences," Emma completed. She looked as exhausted as Liesl felt. "Yes, dear. I know you were raised to think of yourself as terribly important. But if Apollo paid the price for his actions, you can't expect to avoid it. The bill was going to come due eventually. What do you owe?"

"A—" he stuttered, looking wretched. "A child of my blood."

Every one went very quiet. Emma placed a hand on

her stomach — as, Liesl noticed, did two of her three sisters. It might be happy news, if not for the circumstances. After a moment of shocked silence, the room erupted in a rousing shout of protest and condemnation.

Torquay and Tavistock merely watched.

"This," Indigo said wildly to Merry, "is the point in the ballad where he should get struck by lightning."

"Noted," said Meredith Merryweather, poet king.

"I wouldn't let them have *this* child," the Earl was insisting to his wife, gesturing in the general direction of her waist. "Not our —"

"Which child, then, Father?" Retta demanded of him, pushing herself forward to face her father. "Not Gustav the golden heir. Which one of us did you think was expendable enough to sacrifice?"

"Oh," said Liesl, suddenly understanding. It's me." They all stopped, and stared at her. "That's why you sent me here," she said, eyes locked on her father. "You didn't care about the Prima-donna Diamond. It was an excuse to get me to Brightside. Emma left you — probably because you reacted so badly when you found out she was with child. But she unknowingly came to the most dangerous place in the world for her baby. You sent me here, hoping the gods would take me instead."

It was if the crowd were frozen again, caught in a single moment of time. But no, they were just stunned into silence.

The Earl cleared his throat.

"I'm not married, after all," Liesl said calmly. "Not the son and heir. Not the new baby. I'm going spare."

"I wouldn't have thought of it," the Earl sputtered. "If only you'd brought that Duke up to scratch."

"I wasn't aware that my life depended on marrying

him," she shot back. "Are you saying you would have sent *Clytie*, if I was the Duchess of Storm?"

Uncomfortably, the Earl said nothing.

Liesl turned on Torquay and Tavistock. "You don't want me," she said belligerently. "Do you? I'm not good enough for you, either."

The godlings shrugged. "Sacrifices don't count if they're not valued by the one asked to give them up," said Tavistock.

"We do appreciate how tidy you keep your bedroom, miss," offered Torquay. "These artists leave theirs in a terrible state. You're a good house guest. But no. We don't want to kill you. Doesn't mean we won't."

Liesl wanted to laugh and laugh until her throat was raw. She had run out of things to say.

"Does it have to be a child?" spoke up Emma, Countess of Sandwich.

The godlings looked at her.

She stood, with all the majesty of the ancient queens and gods and legendary figures she had modelled during her performance of Classics. "Does the life you are owed have to be a child descended from the Earl?"

"Emma, what are you doing?" Perdita asked in a warning voice.

Tavistock and Torquay smiled in unison; a chilling sight. "It has to hurt," said Tavistock. "He has to give something up. But a life is a life."

Emma nodded. She was at Liesl's side now. She took her hand. For a moment, Liesl remembered what it was like to have a mother who was prepared to be fierce on your behalf. "You are still bound to this household?"

"We are," said Torquay. "The curse might be mortal, but it binds us."

Emma nodded, as if that was what she had expected.

"I expect that means that the Earl and I are safe from you, for now," she considered. "But none of his children are of this household. This is the first visit for all of them. So you probably consider them equally fair game."

Tavistock looked past Liesl and licked her lips. "Some will taste better than others. The ones he'll miss the most."

It was little relief to Liesl that she wasn't high on that list; she hurt all the way down.

"I am the Countess of Sandwich," Emma informed the two godlings. "Mistress of this house. I release you both of your service to Aphrodite Villa. Take your price from the one who owes you the most, and leave the rest of us alone." She squeezed Liesl's hand tightly.

The house shimmered, as a domestic curse long out of fashion removed itself with very little fuss.

Torquay's suit and Tavistock's apron vanished to be replaced with gleaming golden armour. They both held javelins, sharp and menacing.

"Stop this now," demanded the Earl of Sandwich, bearing down upon his wife and daughter. "What do you think you're…" he stopped as the javelins pointed in his direction. "No!" he bellowed, more outraged than afraid. "Not me. You said I was *safe*."

"I'd run if I were you, sir," Torquay advised in his polite butler's voice. "My sister hasn't killed a mortal in centuries. She's been so looking forward to it."

The Earl of Sandwich broke, and ran for the door. After a moment or two, the gods pursued him, vicious grins upon their faces. Sunlight streamed behind them as they ran.

Emma made a noise, half scream and half sob. Liesl held her as she cried. "I'm sorry," Emma said desperately. "I'm sorry, I'm sorry. *Your father*."

Liesl only hugged her harder.

Out of the corner of her eye, she saw her sisters cluster together around Gustav, dazed and shocked.

Perdita moved first, dragging Indigo with her. The two of them came to Emma and Liesl's side, like avenging furies. Perdita swerved at the last minute and embraced Liesl with a grip that proved her upper arm strength. "You're worth a hundred of the lot of them," she growled into Liesl's ear. "I want to wring your father's neck."

"Too late, I think," said Liesl, managing not to laugh or cry.

Anna moved next, shaking herself loose of Retta, Gerda and Gustav. "Thank you," she said to Emma, clasping her hands. "Countess. *Thank you*. You saved my sister's life."

Liesl opened her mouth to say if anything, it was not her life Emma had saved, but Perdita gave her a firm pinch on the hip, and she said nothing.

"You should hate me," Emma insisted, wiping tears from her face.

"I think there's been enough of that, hasn't there?" said Anna.

Retta and Gerda nodded wordlessly.

Gustav looked deeply irritated at them all, but he knew better than to gainsay his three elder sisters.

"Pardon the intrusion on this tender family moment," said Basil Robucks, finally standing up from the piano stool and stretching his legs. "But do you think the house will allow us to leave now? My tailor is convinced I have been abducted… and I have a career to save. If I'm not in Town to be rude about an art exhibition, does it even happen?"

"The house is still a house," said Indigo, looking nervously around the walls and ceiling. "It hasn't turned back into a temple."

"Perhaps Apollo likes it this way," said Merry. "Or

perhaps, being a grove of trees, he has little interest in the whole affair. In my poem, he'll turn up at the end. It would bring a true sense of narrative satisfaction."

Everyone waited for a moment, in case he was right, but there was nothing but the sound of wind in the branches outside.

10

SURELY THERE ARE ABSOLUTELY NO FURTHER SURPRISES AT THIS POINT

FROM: *LADY LIESL BATTENBURG-SEVILLE OF SANDWICH, APHRODITE VILLA, BRIGHTSIDE, THE ISLE OF BATH*

TO: *MRS MNEMOSYNE SEABOURNE, COMFREY COTTAGE, MUDGELY, THE ISLE OF ASTER*

*M*y dear Mrs S,

I hope you are enjoying a calm and peaceful magic-free honeymoon, and to that end shall write little (for now) of what has transpired with me over the last week or so. Let it wait until we are reunited for the full story to unfold.

I have lost the taste for writing letters, and so shall keep this brief.

I am well; I hope you are well. I look forward to visiting you in a few months, when you have settled in nicely to your new home on the Isle of Storm. How convenient that you shall be living so close to Juno, and we can all visit together.

I have discovered I have a talent for solving mysteries, but it is not one I shall chuse to exercise on a daily basis. Mysteries are not for the faint of heart.

I have also discovered something of an interest in modern art. Do you by any chance wish to employ a fresco-painter or sculptor to adorn your new Tempest Manse? I can recommend a rather good one, with whom I hope to spend a great deal of time in the coming months.

You may have heard that my father has recently suffered an unfortunate malady; for family reasons, I have decided not to bother with the upcoming Season. In fact, 'for family reasons', I may never bother with such things again. Party invitations, of course, are always welcome.

However practical it might be to acquire a worthy husband as you and Juno managed so capably, I am in fact no longer in the market for such a purchase. I can't tell you how freeing it is to have realised there are other options in the world.

Your friend,
Perfectly happy for the time being,
Liesl

~

*A*phrodite Villa transformed, one drawing room at a time.

It began with the attics and then, strangely enough, the kitchens. A parlour disappeared. The music room contracted until it was nothing but a harp in a closet.

Walls shifted. Doors disappeared. It happened over a matter of three days.

The Battenburg-Seville siblings were all gone by then,

returned to their various homes and estates. Gustav was the last to leave, caught in the great uncertainty of whether or not he had become an Earl.

Finally, a letter arrived informing the family that George, Earl of Sandwich, had been found wandering the grounds of a most exclusive and expensive sanitarium, suffering from mild amnesia and three open javelin wounds. The gods had, in this case, decided to be merciful.

Their mercy, however, included the retrieval and unravelling of the Earl's many wishes. And so the house reverted quite slowly to form, becoming the Temple of Apollo once more.

No one was as surprised as Gustav that he felt relieved rather than disappointed to still be an heir and not an Earl. He hurried off immediately in a train-bound curricle to return to Battenburg Abbey and check on the state of the roof.

On the third day after the house began to unshape itself, Liesl awoke to discover that her bedroom no longer existed, and she had been lying on green grass for several hours. After wandering around the restored temple, she discovered that the breakfast room was still intact, including Perdita's fresco of the nymphs and the dryads.

Mrs Pennance, who prided herself on being able to cook up a feast with only a small oil burner in the back of a theatre dressing room, managed reasonably well with the surviving wood stove, and thus there were sausages and eggs for breakfast, if no home-baked pastries.

Emma, a little green around the gills from her delicate condition, managed to struggle to the breakfast table and greet her remaining guests. Basil was already gone, having hightailed it back to Town ahead of them all.

Indigo and Merry showed no sign of leaving Emma's side. Liesl knew how they felt. And as for Perdita…

"Your beautiful artwork!" Emma burst out over a superior cup of tea, which was all she could manage to keep down apart from a piece or two of Mrs Pennance's shortbread. "I'm so sorry, Perdita. Such a waste."

"Not as much as you might think," said the artist. "Haven't you noticed? They've kept most of them, though there's been a certain amount of rearranging across the temple walls. I plan to let all future patrons know they are competing with Apollo himself."

"Still no portals," Indigo said with a tragic air. "Why couldn't we have offended gods with a more modern attitude towards magic?"

"All those spells going wrong was the first sign there was something odd going on around here," Liesl said, adding several toasted muffins to her plate.

"And I don't understand that at all!" complained Indigo. "Magic works in temples. Doesn't it? Otherwise I should never have been able to use concealing charms on all those playscripts I read as a child, instead of paying attention at services in my home village."

"And yet," said Perdita. "I couldn't stick an enchantment to a wall in this house for the life of me."

"I think," said Liesl. "There was just so much huge magic washing around — the presence of Apollo in the trees, plus Torquay and Tavistock. Perhaps the magic didn't go right for the same reason that you can't boil a cup of tea while underwater, or taste a cup of lemonade you just spilled into the ocean."

"Or," said Emma pointedly. "Perhaps, after my husband managed to put a family curse on two gods and stole their temple, they decided mortal magic should be interrupted every time we tried to use it."

"They're both good explanations," Merry decided. "I expect the butler is too busy to pop back and answer any follow up questions. I'll just have to pick which one I prefer, for my poem." He drank deeply of a bowl of coffee. "Lucky no one did try to install a portal in this place, considering the erratic nature of magic in the presence of Apollo," he mused. We might have all ended up in Bohemia."

"I've been worse places," said Liesl. When he held his bowl of coffee in her general direction, she gently chinked her teacup against it.

~

Some time later that day:

"Liesl, you're still here," said Emma, sounding harried. "Are you finished packing? There's a train at six, which we should just be able to make if we set off by curricle soon…"

"The temple packed for me," said Liesl. "Including the family betrothal ring and the Seville tiara, by the way, which it decided belonged in my carpet bag instead of yours."

"Oh, you'd better keep them. I don't want to be accused of taking more than my share!"

The unravelling of wishes had hit Emma harder than the rest of them. Her memories of the last six years were intact, but some layers had been washed away… such as the memory of how exactly she had agreed to marry George in the first place, giving up her career without a thought.

She had several appointments with divorce lawyers specialising in heritage and inheritance law coming up in Town over the next few weeks. Liesl had agreed to stand as a witness against her father's actions if Emma needed it — as, almost surprisingly, had all four of her elder siblings.

"Wait," Emma said suddenly, digging in her own bag. "This one's definitely for you. Add it to the pile."

To Liesl's astonishment, an enormous white gold necklace slithered into her outstretched hand. The central setting included a large diamond teardrop, twelve amethyst, and twenty four pink sapphires. The Primadonna Diamond.

"What," she said flatly.

"It was never missing," Emma confessed. "I sent a letter to some old theatre friend, asking them to contact the Earl and tell him it had been seen across various jewellers in Town."

"What!" Liesl exclaimed, rather more furiously than before.

"I'm sorry, dearest." Emma gave her a motherly hug. "It was the only way I could think to get his attention. I'm not sure quite, in fact, that seemed so important at the time, but I felt quite unsettled being here without him. Now, of course, I know why that was. I didn't mean to bring all this down on you. The divorce or the angry gods."

Liesl gave up, and hugged her in return. "You've lost more than the rest of us. Are you sure you don't want to be a Countess any more? We can make sure Father doesn't bother you…"

"Oh," said Emma, with an odd expression on her face. "No offence, Liesl, but the prospect of not being the Countess of Sandwich is the happiest thing that has happened to me since the time I was cast as Andronica at the Old Poseidon. I'll get to live my life again. And we'll still be family, if you want."

Her hand ghosted over the slight bump at the front of her dress. Barely noticeable unless you knew to look for it.

"Of course I want," Liesl said indignantly. "I'm an

excellent big sister. I'll bully Clytie to send you a reference if you like."

Emma laughed; a lovely sound. She looked like a free woman. "So, the train?"

"I think I might wait and come back later," said Liesl. "Tomorrow, or the next day. Whenever's convenient."

"Oh, I see," said Emma with a knowing smile. "Perdita's staying a little longer too."

There was no reason at all why Liesl should blush at that, and yet…

⁓

*B*y the following morning, barely anyone was left in the Temple of Apollo that had once masqueraded as Aphrodite Villa. Mrs Pennance had left on the same train as Emma, Merry and Indigo. Bets the tweeny and Bert the stable lad had returned to their enormous Brightside families.

Amie remained, of course. She was occupying herself for the morning on the promenade, with one last toss at the coconut shy and one last toffee apple. She deserved a day off before having to face curricles and travel-sickness again.

(Perhaps the toffee apple was a mistake they would both regret.)

Liesl found Perdita in the breakfast room, examining the fresco with a critical eye. "I think I can get the charm to work this time," she muttered. "Now there aren't as many gods cluttering up the place."

"You mean, apart from the god inhabiting the trees outside?" Liesl said. "Leave it. It's perfect."

Perdita took a deep breath, and gave her one of those

warm smiles. "You stayed another night. Not fleeing back to civilisation quite yet?"

"Nothing to flee to," said Liesl, hoping that didn't make her sound too pathetic. "My family have scattered, my friends are all married… and I have no idea what to do with myself next." She knew what she was not doing. She was not submitting herself to the formalities of another Season. Apart from that… well. She awaited inspiration.

Perdita continued to peer at her fresco, prodding at the various nymphs and dryads. "You were terribly fierce in that drawing room," she said. "As if you'd been solving mysteries and challenging the gods all your life."

"I think I'm done with that," Liesl replied. "Once was enough. What about you? Still wildly inspired?"

Everyone else had been in such a rush to get away from the former villa. Should she be concerned that Perdita still lingered? (Should she be concerned that Liesl, too, was not quite ready to leave yet? She had only written one letter that morning, which seemed a normal amount of letter-writing for a lady of her station. But it was hard to be sure what 'normal' was after the last week of her life.)

Perdita turned to face her. For once, there was uncertainty in her face. Her glorious cat's eyes were dim. "Will I still be good enough if I leave this place?" she burst out. "I don't think I ever really believed in my skill as an artist until I was here, under this roof. And none of it was real."

"You were good enough to get kicked out of the Royal Academy for unladylike behaviour," said Liesl, in an attempt to cheer her up. "Perdita. Do you not know how brilliant you are? I'm sure I heard something about a royal commission…"

Perdita shook off her moment uncertainty, or masked it well enough. "And you, Lady Liesl? Did the presence of Apollo inspire you towards any art form in particular?

Scrapbooking? Watercolours? I've always thought mosaics would be rather fun. So much smashing of tiles with a hammer…"

"I wrote letters," Liesl sighed. She hadn't admitted it out loud to anyone yet. "To my friends, new and old. My sister and my mamma and grandmamma — both dead, the last two. It's the first time I've been honest with them all. About my life and my fears and my future. I've spent my whole life playing into this idea of what was expected of me. Somehow, in this house, for the first time I can't lie to myself about what I want."

Perdita looked intrigued. Here, surrounded by walls covered with her own artwork, she had eyes only for Liesl. "You didn't write me any letters. I'm quite offended. I suppose you'll have to tell me what you want in person…"

Liesl kissed her.

It was not a good kiss, though in truth Liesl had little to compare it to. In her world, young ladies had kisses bestowed upon them (once a formal courtship was far enough along). They did not take the initiative, and they certainly did not hurl themselves wildly upon acquaintances at the drop of a hat.

(Apart from Dimity Briggs-Weston, of course, who ended up marrying her footman, which everyone thought was best under the circumstances.)

It occurred to Liesl once the kiss was already underway that this was dreadfully awkward, and really one should talk about these things first, she had always hated being pounced upon herself, and now she had done that exact thing to this lovely woman who was only being polite, and…

The kiss changed. Now that Perdita had recovered from those first few startled seconds, she took control. One hand slid against Liesl's back, capturing a handful of white muslin. The other hand cradled her cheek.

And oh, it was not a bad kiss any more. Not by any stretch of the imagination. Nor was it awkward. It was…

The best surprise so far.

~

Some time later, they walked in and around the laurel trees, hand-in-hand, whiling away a pleasant hour or so before Amie returned, and the three of them set off back to the nearest portal by way of a train ride sandwiched between two curricles.

Liesl wasn't even dreading it any more. Not with a travel companion such as this. They were heading to the Isle of Town — Liesl to her family's usual apartment at Court, Perdita to a boarding house for wayward artists which had the convenience of nearby studio space. Thanks to the magical convenience of portals, which had quite taken over the Teacup Isles, they would be able to see as much of each other as they wished.

And oh, Liesl wished.

She didn't even mind that she would be in Town for the Season, as she intended to avoid all society parties except those where her presence was especially demanded by friends. She was looking forward to a slightly different social scene, this time around. One with gallery openings and poetry recitals instead of balls and assemblies.

"I want to learn watercolours," she said aloud, then gave a suspicious glare at the laurel trees overhead. "At least, I think that's what I want. I'll check in with the idea again when we've put more distance between us and a Certain Someone."

Perdita laughed, a throaty, sensuous sound. "My

darling," she said. "It's a slippery slope. I started with watercolours, and look at me now."

"I think you're marvellous," said Liesl, warm all over at being called Perdita's anything, let along 'darling'. "I also think I want to kiss you again."

Perdita leaned against the tree, careless of the possibility it might be a slumbering god. "Practice makes perfect," she said invitingly.

Liesl clasped both of her hands and leaned in. "I don't need to be be perfect," she said. "But some things are worth practicing regardless."

"I couldn't agree more," said Perdita.

11

SIX MONTHS LATER

Excerpt from The Teacup Weekly Art Supplement, By Agatha Knowles

NYMPHS, GODS AND REVENGE AT THE SEASIDE!!!

A new art exhibit has set the art world buzzing this winter, at the Siddal Gallery in the North Quarter. Miss Perdita Cholmondley, infamous painter and sculptor (who was interviewed for this publication last year during The Great Pygmalion Academy Scandal) has launched her new triptych: *Daphne's Escape*, depicting an unusual take on a classic mythological tale across three eight-foot canvases.

In the paintings, the nymph Daphne is pursued by the god Apollo, but in a surprising turn of events, he is transformed into a grove of laurel trees by his vengeful sister Artemis, instead of Daphne's father turning her into a tree to escape the god's lusts. Quite unusually, the figures are clothed in modern dress, with the background setting of a busy seaside town rather than a more traditional forest glade; indeed, in the final painting, we we see Daphne and Artemis enjoying an evening promenade together along a pier of diverse amusements, with the laurel trees (scene of the crime) far in the distance. The basket of strawberries and cream carried between the two women, and the tilt of their faces towards each other, is suggestive of a mutual romantic encounter.

A recent soirée to celebrate Miss Cholmondley's work was attended by an unusual number of noble patrons, including the Duke and Duchess of Storm, Lord and Lady Chisholm, Lady L. of Sandwich and, in a startling return to society, Mrs Emma Lamb, (div.) former Countess of Sandwich and current star of the comic opera *Tales of Bohemia* at the Ophelian Pleasure Gardens.

Other noteworthy guests in attendance: Miss I. Larkin, understudy to Mrs Lamb; Mrs P. Daze, celebrated lady novelist; Mr M. Merryweather, author of the recently bestselling epic poem *Apollo Swallows His Children*, and Mr & Mrs M. Seabourne.

Speeches were given by Miss Cholmondley as well as Mr Basil Robucks, the famous dandy and arbiter of men's fashion who was once described by the Count of Nemesis as "the only gentleman who knows better than a cravat, how it should be tied."

Mr Robucks declared Miss Cholmondley's work to be groundbreaking and original, and made several rather risqué references to strawberries which shall not be repeated in this supplement.

The Palace has confirmed that her Royal Majesty

Queen Aud will be celebrated by an official bust in rose marble, sculpted by Miss Cholmondley.

Turn to our Fashion Supplement for sketches of the best outfits from this exclusive event! Including a fold out pattern of the Duchess of Storm's Expanding Maternity Pelisse, and close detail sketches of Mr Robucks' folded pocket square.

Turn to our Theatre Pages for a glowing review of *Tales of Bohemia*.

For the best strawberries and cream, visit the Continental Tearooms on the River Scamander. Serving summer fruits all year around, thanks to the new advancements in preservation enchantments.

Have you offended the gods lately? Visit the Pantheon Temple on Ruskin Street to discuss your options.

THE END

GLOSSARY OF THE TEACUP ISLES

HONEYMOON EDITION

- Aphrodite, goddess of love
- Aphrodite Villa — a luxurious, ironically-named holiday home on the cliffs overlooking the town of Brightside, on the Isle of Bath.
- Apollo, god of art, music and inspiration
- Artemis, goddess of the hunt
- Aster, Isle of — a minor island within the Lordship of Manticore, famous for its lack of magic, its splendid holiday lake and its country ways
- Bath, Isle of — one of the Teacup Isles: a holiday destination with healing waters
- Battenburg Abbey — ancestral home of the Earl of Sandwich and the Battenburg-Seville family.
- Belverdene — an exclusive club in Town reserved for ladies awarded a coveted voucher by one of the patrons.
- Brightside — a seaside town on the unfashionable coast of the Isle of Bath.

- Bumbleton Palace — the Queen's country palace, on the minor Isle of Aster
- Continent, the — an extremely large island, beyond the Lyric Sea, foreign but fashionable
- Continental Tearooms, the — first establishment in the Teacup Isles to advertise portals for ladies.
- Court of Lords, the — one of the two official government bodies of the Teacup Isles; the aristocratic one
- Croquet, the new — a jolly game involving young ladies, sticks, balls and creative sorcery
- Curricle — a two-wheeled carriage driven with two horses; no footmen required
- Delphi College — a magical university, mostly reserved for the very wealthy (and a small number of scholarship students)
- Dormouse, Isle of — one of the Teacup Isles: a barony and a source of rather good tea
- Drowned Grisella — a play about a tragic young lady and several very unsympathetic men.
- Gentlewoman, the — a lady's magazine full of fashion plates, cosmetic recipes and discreet employment advertisements
- Ices — a delicious frozen dessert made from flavoured custards and cordials; terribly expensive in summer, and really quite reasonably priced in winter
- Luncheon — a light midday meal often enjoyed by ladies, and occasionally hijacked by gentlemen
- Lyric Sea, the — home to the Teacup Isles
- Madeleines — tiny curved sponge cakes, baked

in cast iron moulds with a specific shell-like
design
- Magisters — mysterious working magicians,
blamed and/or credited for all manner of
sinister goings on
- Manticore, Isle of — one of the Teacup Isles: a
lordship
- Manse — a house provided for the senior
temple priest or magister of a town or village,
and their family
- Masque — a costume ball in which all
participants are expected to be masked
- Memory, Isle of — one of the Teacup Isles:
quiet, peaceful
- Midsummer Night's Occurrence — a popular
tragic play by Sir Dilles Blightweather, about
the Midnight Fairy, tricked into loving a mortal
with the head of a donkey. Everyone dies at the
end, except the donkey.
- Mudgely — a lakeside village on the Isle of
Aster, within walking distance of Bumbleton
Palace
- Muslin — the lightest possible of cotton fabric,
very fashionable and worn by ladies in pale
white and cream colours
- Name day — far more important than
birthdays, with better presents
- Ophelian Pleasure Gardens, the — a public
park by day and premiere venue for
entertainments by night, on the Isle of Town
- Parliament of Gentles, the — one of the two
official government bodies of the Teacup Isles;
the slightly more egalitarian one
- Portals — a magical method of stepping

through magical gateways. Restricted to male use until very recently, thanks to a revolutionary campaign led by a certain Miss Mnemosyne Seabourne

- Pygmalion Academy — a prestigious institute of sculpture
- Queen of Hearts — a comic opera about a tyrannical queen who executes all her husbands
- Ratafia — a fortified wine, flavoured with almond, spice or orange blossom; or, in a pinch, any fruity punch that is also alcoholic
- Sandwich, Isle of — one of the Teacup Isles: an earldom
- Season — that part of the year when unmarried nobility are positively encouraged to court each other in dramatic fashion: begins with the opening of the Court of Lords at the end of autumn, continues with the opening of the Parliament of Gentles in midwinter, and can be extended by garden parties and house parties well into spring if your mamma is steadfast enough
- Sensibility, the Isle of — one of the Teacup Isles: a duchy. The first isle to legalise same sex marriage and adoption
- Shellwich Standing — the Seabourne family home, on the isle of Memory
- Spellcracker — a professional person whose specialty is the removal, shielding and dissolving of unwanted magics
- Storm, Isle of — one of the Teacup Isles: a dukedom.
- Storm Bolt — the Duke of Storm's townhouse, featuring four secret passages, twelve maids,

three libraries and the best of all possible butlers

- Storm North — the Duke of Storm's country seat
- Swan-shaped boats — once the only polite manner of travel between islands for those of the female persuasion; now desperately old-fashioned
- Sympathetic magic — a minor form of spellcraft, using objects (often charmed) to form small but significant shifts in reality, will or marital status
- Tempest Manse — a newly built home for the Duke of Storm's spellcracker, and his wife
- Town, Isle of — the centre of most social activity in the Teacup Isles, featuring the Isle of Court
- Wistworia Palace — a palace in Town

ABOUT THE AUTHOR

Tansy Rayner Roberts is an award-winning Australian science fiction and fantasy author who never wears corsets or muslin. She lives with her family in Tasmania and has been known to pick up the occasional embroidery hoop.

- Listen to Tansy on Sheep Might Fly, a podcast where she reads aloud her stories as audio serials.
- Read Tansy's stories before anyone else when you pledge to her Patreon: patreon.com/tansyrr
- What tea is Tansy drinking? Find out when you subscribe to her excellent newsletter.
- Follow Tansy on Amazon or Bookbub so you never miss a release.

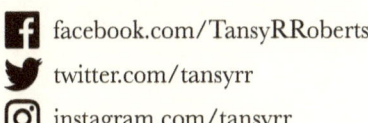

facebook.com/TansyRRoberts

twitter.com/tansyrr

instagram.com/tansyrr

ALSO BY TANSY RAYNER ROBERTS

Tea & Sympathetic Magic

There's nothing more dangerous than an eligible duke...

Every eligible young lady of the Teacup Isles wants to marry the
Duke of Storm, except Miss Mnemosyne Seabourne, who is
quite content on the shelf, thank you very much. All she wants is
a quiet life and a good book.

At a house party full of ruthless debutantes willing to employ
sneaky sympathetic magic to win a husband of quality, Mneme
joins forces with an enigmatic spellcracker to rescue the duke
from being married against his will.

Can Mneme save the Duke of Storm without becoming his
bride? Will this caper ruin her reputation forever? Can teacups
and hedgehogs be used as projectile weapons in emergencies?
Why are attractive men more devastating when they roll up their
sleeves?

If you enjoy Regency house parties, witty romantic banter and
high society sorcery, you'll adore this magical comedy of
manners cosy mystery novella.

The Frost Fair Affair

Our heroine stumbles across a precarious plot while printing political pamphlets...

Thanks to last Season's scandal involving her family, Miss Mnemosyne Seabourne is officially notorious. Wintering in Town, she hopes to use her new celebrity to campaign about the unfair restriction on portal travel for ladies... while being quietly courted by a certain handsome spellcracker.

As the river freezes over and a spectacular Frost Fair sets up on the ice, Mneme finds herself beset by secret societies, spies and sneaky saboteurs. Who stole her political pamphlets? Who is leaving dead bodies around printing presses for anyone to find?

Mr Thornbury knows more than he's letting on. If she can't trust the man she hoped to marry, Mneme is just going to have to unravel the mystery for herself, quick enough to save both of their lives.

If you enjoy vintage spy adventures, flirtatious couples and cosy sleigh rides, you'll adore this exciting sequel novella to *Tea and Sympathetic Magic*.

Spellcracker's Honeymoon

Our honeymooning heroine must unmask a magical murderer.

Happily married, Mrs Mnemosyne Seabourne travels to an island of no magic, for a relaxing honeymoon with her new husband Thornbury.

But the magic-free Isle of Aster is not what it seems. There's a monster roaming the hills, a royal scandal brewing on the horizon, and (of course!) an impossible, magical murder to be solved.

On the night of the Midsummer Masque at the Queen's country palace, Thornbury goes missing, leaving Mneme to unravel a web of secrets and lies involving her own husband.

Who could commit magical murder on an island with no magic? Only a spellcracker...

If you enjoy cozy magical mysteries, glamorous masquerade balls and the art of saucy letter writing, you'll love the third Teacup Magic novella.

Castle Charming

In this fairy tale kingdom, the royals of Castle Charming have always been cursed. What will it take to heal their family, and survive the magical threat overwhelming their land?

The cruel truth behind fairy godmothers.

Disaster princes cursed to dance all night.

A sleeping spell with a taste for royal blood.

A giant attack beanstalk.

A powerful magical princess who could destroy them all.

Castle Charming is an enormously fun collection of LGBTQ+ fairy tale adventure novellas.